Romance under aquarius

Stargazing Series, Book One

DANIELLE JACKS

Danielle Jacks

Romance under Aquarius is written in British English. This book is the work of fiction. Any names, characters, places, and events are either creations of the author's imagination or used fictitiously. Any similarities are purely coincidental.

Collaboration Organiser: Phoenix Book Promo

Editor: Karen Sanders

Proofreader: Rebecca Martin

Cover design: Shower of Schmidt

Formatting: Phoenix Book Promo

Starsign Credit: The Zodiac City

Aquarius

She does her best to let her mind be her biggest asset, thinking, creating and the like, but she is also the rebel and may lose her vision when trying to make a point.

Boring and clingy people annoy her.

She is not afraid to be herself and values opinions as long as hers are heard as well

She loves hard but doesn't always know how to show it.

Romance under Aquarius is book 1# of the Stargazing series, a 12-book series of standalones.

Kasper

What would you do for your dying brother?
Would you travel the world and swim to the deepest depths?
If I told you Greek mythology speaks of a water healer under the zodiac sign of Aquarius, would you consider going after it?

Maris

What would you do if you found out your fiancé was cheating on you?
Would you fight your father's decision to have you marry him?

If I told you your opinion wouldn't change a thing,
would you fight to be heard or maybe run away?

Pasha

What would you do if the only person you loved was
intended for your best friend?
Would you sacrifice your own happiness for theirs?
If I told you your future following others' rules would
make you miserable, would you step in line?

Ryn

What would you do if you found out you could be king
but you'd have to marry someone you didn't love?
Would you try to make it work?
If I told you the princess is destined for more than you
can offer, would you help her?

SCORPIO
LIBRA
VIRGO

Prologue

AQUARIUS IS REPRESENTED BY THE WATER HEALER

"Legend has it the lost city of Atlantis will be discovered by a member of my family. The Colombo family," I say to the beautiful lady sitting on my lap.

I tell this story to all the pretty girls in Haiti because I love the Caribbean island, and I need it to hold some truth. Conning rich people out of money is how I afford to stay here, and this is where I need to be. The Marriot Port-Au Prince is one of my favourite hotels, and it's why

I chose Lara as my date for tonight. She's booked the hotel for her stay in Haiti.

"Tell me about your last treasure hunt, Kyle." She seductively bites her lip.

The first rule of making someone believe a story is to keep it simple. Kyle is not my name, but it begins with a K.

"Imagine days at sea with only a gallon of water left and the sun beating down on your skin like a punishment from the gods. I was almost ready to give up. My mouth was as dry as sandpaper, and my energy was low from lack of nourishment. I thought I'd failed. My time was up, and I couldn't carry on." I pause for dramatic effect. "But then a magpie plucked a small ring box from the sea and dropped it right by my feet."

"A magpie?" she asks with a frown.

I chuckle lightly. I easily become bored with spinning the same bullshit, so even though it's risky, I like to test the limits. "You know those birds like shiny things," I say in a condescending tone. Women seem to respond well to me being an asshole.

"Well yes. In England, I've seen many of them, but not here." Her voice is wavering like she's unsure of herself.

"Have you been out into the deep sea while in Haiti?" I ask, trying to sound interested.

Lara is at least five years younger than me and doesn't seem like the fishing type. At twenty, I probably didn't know the difference between a carp and a haddock either. Now, most of my diet consists of what I can catch on the end of a rod.

"I went to a party on a yacht." Her little pouty lips smile like this is something that will impress. If only I could be so carefree. I can't remember the last time I went out just to have fun.

"Aw, honey. You're too precious to see the magpies." She adjusts her position on my knee, and I'm close to losing my target. These women like my bad attitude, but maybe I've drifted too far with this one. "All I'm saying is, you have too many important things to do to look at boring animals. You've worked hard to get this holiday. You deserve a relaxing break."

The tension in her shoulders evaporates. "Yes, you're right. Carry on with your story." She smiles again, satisfied with my answer.

"The ring box was made of silver, and that's what attracted the bird. I dived into the sea to take a closer look. Sure enough, like a shiny beacon, there was a whole box of jewels. The days and nights I'd spent in the rough sea paid off when I took the treasure to the museum. They were so grateful for the donation and confirmed it was from the lost city of Atlantis."

Rich people like old money. I always mention a charity so they think I'm one of them.

"I thought that was just a myth."

I push my shaggy blonde hair out of my face. "Did you dream of unicorns and mermaids as a little girl?"

"Sure."

"What if I told you one of those two things is real?"

"Part of growing up is letting go of those fantasies." She doesn't look convinced.

"Only if you want to."

The sparkle in her eyes says she's imagining something she wants, and maybe I can give it to her. The illusion of a holiday romance with a rich entrepreneur is what most women want when they come to Haiti, and I don't think my companion is any different.

"You have an interesting outlook on the world and an amazing job. Will you take me to the museum to see the treasure?"

There it is. She's putty in my hands. Time is something I can't offer. "Sorry, no. I can't. We only have tonight. I'm going on a long expedition tomorrow."

"Aw." She pouts. "I don't fly home to Essex for another week."

"We'd better make the most of the time we have." I take her glass of wine from her hand, placing it on the table before kissing her.

"Let's go upstairs," she says.

I give her a wicked smile and she falls straight into my trap. "Lead the way."

She takes hold of my arm and we walk to her room. As we enter, I quickly scope the room for its inventory. I spend the next hour pleasuring her until she finally falls asleep. I wipe down the surfaces and get rid of every trace of my presence. Then I help myself to her diamonds, rubies, and cash. Once I have everything she can offer, I make my exit.

The streets of Haiti are lined with poverty hidden away from tourists. People only want to see the beauty and not the cruel world hidden beneath the surface. I visit the local shop and buy some fresh bread and vegetables. I take some of them to the orphanage, where I leave it inside the door before heading home.

"You're a disgrace. Dad would be ashamed if he could see you right now," my older brother, Owen, says as I empty my pockets onto our small round table.

"We've got to eat." I'm not proud I have to steal, but I don't have another option. Fresh fish is the only thing I can get for free, but it's not enough to survive on or pay our rent on our apartment in the metropolitan area of Port-au-Prince.

"You need to make an honest living. When I agreed to come here seven months ago, I didn't think it would make you a criminal." We both worked for a tech giant back home, but we didn't realise we should've been saving every penny rather than blowing it all on insignificant things. Here, those skills are useless because we don't even have a smartphone between us. We're back to basics with a barely functional old Nokia.

"I can't work and take the jon boat out. If I'm on land, I need to be in the library doing research. I'm going to follow another lead tomorrow."

Lara had a guidebook that contained a picture of some rocks I want to locate. I have the coordinates, and once it's light, I'll set sail.

"We should go back to London. The doctors might've missed something." He coughs into his hand.

Modern medicine can't help us. Nothing short of a miracle will work now.

"Pancreatic cancer doesn't just disappear. You can't be cured by science." I'm a desperate man willing to go to extreme lengths. A pain tugs at my heart. I can't lose him. "The lost city of Atlantis is somewhere near these Caribbean Islands, I can feel it. Just give me more time."

The doctors warned us he'd be lucky to survive until the end of the year, but I won't give up until his last breath.

"God waits for nobody." He coughs again, and I

help him into his chair. His once lean body now looks too thin, but I push away my worry.

"I'm not giving up. The research I found on the zodiac signs looks promising. I'll find the jug of Aquarius, and using its healing water, I'll make you better." I can't hide the desperation as it seeps into my words. He closes his eyes, and I'm as tired as he is. I find a blanket to wrap around him before kissing his head. "I'll save you." I pat his hand, but he doesn't move. His breathing slows as he drifts into sleep.

I pick up the tatty old book that inspired our trip and read the passage that has given me hope for the last six months. 'A land dweller and a fish will heal the world. One sip from the Aquarius jug will heal time.' It seemed like nonsense when I first discovered it, but there are references to the legend throughout history. Ganymede's story of being the water healer is one I have to trust and believe. I think the Aquarius jug can turn back the clock and bring youth back to cells. I'm not talking about a strong anti-wrinkle cream. I think it can cure cancer. Breaking down the quote, if I can find the fish, maybe I can be the land dweller. Then together, we can find the jug. My brother's life literally depends on it.

Once in the bathroom, I run the tap. It's hard to see my reflection in the dirty mirror. I rinse my hair before wiping the glass. My sun-kissed skin isn't from days of relaxing by the beach. It's from the hours I've spent in the ocean. My blue eyes look tired, and I look older than my twenty-five years. I need to save my brother. It's the only thing I'm living for. The lost city of Atlantis may only be a fantasy for some, but I have to believe it's real and mermaids live there. I think the fish in question is a mermaid, and the city is their home. I have to find the water bearer or it will kill us both.

SCORPIO
LIBRA
VIRGO

Chapter One

AQUARIUS WAS ONE OF THE FIRST ZODIAC CONSTELLATIONS TO BE DISCOVERED

Maris

Angler fish look beautiful when it's dark and only their headlights are glowing. They dance across the open space as the ocean carnival begins with harmonic music. This is one of my favourite nights of the year, and I struggle to contain my excitement. One of the fishes opens its bioluminescent eyes and bites into the pink balloon in front of it. Luminous colour spurts from the angler's mouth, lighting up the sea like a firework. Four more fish follow their leader and pretty bursts of fuchsia shoot across the water.

Twirling seahorses glide up and down when the lights come back on. Vibrant shades of purple surround us, and I squeeze my best friend Pasha's hand with excitement. "See! I knew you could pull it off," I whisper.

"I'm glad you think so. I really want to join the royal events committee." Pasha has always wanted a job in the performing arts sector, and now we're eighteen, she's making her aspirations known.

"You're a natural," I say as the music becomes louder and faster.

"If the princess recommends me, I might have a better chance," she hints.

I try to applaud her work the best I can, but it's her dedication that will give her a fighting chance of getting the job. For some reason, my father isn't her biggest fan, and it makes it difficult for me to recommend her. "I'll tell a few of the royals how good you are. Look at the starfish! Even they look great this year." They tend to miss their cue, but their timings are perfect. The show finishes with all different types of fish swirling around until the music cuts off and they all scram.

My father, King Cyrus, shouts, "Welcome to the ocean carnival. The festival is now open for all to enjoy." He spreads his arms wide. The merpeople swim towards the entertainment, leaving us watching them.

"I'm hoping to see Ryn tonight," I say to Pasha, smiling and feeling giddy.

"When's your father going to announce your engagement?" Pasha asks, but her smile from the carnival has vanished.

"Don't be sad. We'll still be able to hang out." Since we finished school, we don't see each other as much, but I try to make time for her.

"I know. I just wish we could choose who we marry. I'd like to have a mate I love."

"Don't feel bad for me. Ryn seems like a nice merman."

"Yes, but you hardly know him."

"That will change once we're married."

She frowns but tries to cover it with a fake smile. I don't know what's got into her lately; she doesn't seem to be herself. It could be the stress of organising the opening sequence for the carnival, but I'm unsure. Every time I try to ask her about it, she changes the subject. "Let's go get some clams," she says, tugging me forward.

"Okay." We swim into the marketplace and help ourselves to the food trays.

Butterflies start in the pit of my stomach when I realise who's nearby. My betrothed is talking to one of his friends, and I allow myself the pleasure of admiring him. His thick bronze tail compliments my gold, womanly curves. He's like the dark to my light. I have dirty blonde hair, whereas his hair is dark brown. I have one picture of us from New Year which shows how perfect we look together. I can imagine our beautiful merbabies completing our portrait. I've had a crush on him since school but only admired him from afar. It would be improper for me to do anything else. When we were matched as a couple, I couldn't believe my luck. I knew my suitor would be from royal blood, but I had no clue it would be him. We haven't spent much time alone yet, as father keeps me on a tight leash, but I'm optimistic we'll be great.

"Ryn's looking this way. I wonder if he liked my entertainment," Pasha says. A warm blush covers her face. She's trying so hard to get the job. I want to help her with the committee by making sure they saw her work.

"When I get a few minutes in privacy with him, I'll put in a good word," I say.

If Pasha's lucky, Ryn might mention her role to his mother. She works on the royal board. We smile at him and he waves. It's been over a week since I got time with him. My father keeps a close watch on me when he can, and it's not acceptable for me to be seen without a female escort. I've tried to bring Pasha to one of our get-togethers, but it felt awkward.

We've been staring a while before he comes over. "Ladies," he says.

"Hi, Ryn," I almost sing out. It's okay to have a crush on your future husband, right?

"Hey," Pasha says hesitantly. I try to ignore whatever has her on edge.

"The show was great," Ryn says, making Pasha blush.

"Be sure to recommend her to the committee," I say.

"My mother saw the performance." His eyes never leave Pasha's, which I hope reassures her.

"Have you tried the clam?" I ask, offering one from my tray.

"Actually, I'm hungry for something else."

What does that mean? He isn't looking at me, and I don't think he's flirting.

"I could take a swim with you." I smile brightly, but my bubble bursts quickly.

"I have to go, but we'll catch up later." He hugs us goodbye, then leaves.

"I wish we had more time together," I say with a sigh.

"He might not be everything you're expecting him to be," Pasha says.

"You might be feeling glum, but don't pull me down." I pout.

"Sorry, Maris. I'm having a strange night." She pauses. "I've just remembered there's somewhere I need to be."

"Oh, okay then," I say, but she's already swimming away. It's odd that she has to leave her debut event. I shake off the negative energy jumping around in my stomach.

My father is sitting on his events throne, and I swim to join him.

"Are you enjoying the carnival delights?" he asks. His warm smile settles me, and I try to forget my friends' weird vibes.

"Yes. Pasha did a fabulous job with the opening ceremony," I say, although I feel like that information is on a script. I've said it so many times.

"You know I don't like you hanging out with that girl," he says sternly.

"If only you'd give her a chance, you would see she's kind and caring."

"You should be socializing with royals like yourself."

"I don't need to now you've chosen me a suitor." I'm impressed he picked Ryn. He isn't the highest-ranking of the royal families, but he is the most handsome.

"Once you're married, you will have no choice but to find your close circle of allies."

"Father, you're wrong. All these merfolk have always looked after me."

"Not everything's as it seems, and I hope you don't find out the hard way."

Why is everyone talking in riddles today?

"Don't be such a worrywart." We enjoy the rest of the evening together before I head to my room at bedtime. My dad is overprotective, but I know it's because he cares.

Once the kingdom has settled, I sneak out. I'm careful not to be seen as that would damage my reputation, but I love spending time alone in the wide ocean. I take my usual path along the coral and up into the shallow water. Atlantis looks so small from up here.

When I reach the surface, it's dark. There's something beautiful about the moon, even if my father forbids me from coming up here. Apparently, it's dangerous, but I'm always careful. Just like the sea, the land seems calm. I pass through the harbour, free a couple of shrimps from a net, and watch romance blossom on the beach between the humans.

The hours pass me by and the sun begins to rise. The reflection shimmers over the water and the first couple of fishermen are already approaching, which means it's my time to leave. Now I don't have the shadows to hide in.

A human man is walking towards a tatty boat. His

facial features are hard but not unkind. I watch him climb on board the rotting wood as I leave the harbour. Why doesn't he make a new one? It's hard to understand humans, but I can't exactly ask him.

I decide to make one last stop before returning to my room. It's a secret place I haven't told anyone about, except my best friend. I found the helm of a pirate ship just over a year ago, which is sitting on top of an unopened treasure box. It's silly, but I like to think of it as Pandora's treasure, and opening it would be wrong. It doesn't belong to me and I don't know the sacrifice made for the treasure to be left here.

Sinking down, I return to the deep blue ocean and welcome the colours of the coral. Plants on land don't compare to the beauties under the sea. After a tricky passage through the rocks, I locate the wheel, taking a stance behind it.

A noise in the distance has me diving down toward the treasure and out of sight. Laughter echoes around the water as I clutch my chest. I'd recognise that voice anywhere. It's Pasha. I spring up from my hiding spot. The smile on my face quickly fades. She's with Ryn, and they look over-friendly. Their body language is almost flirtatious, and my mind fills with confusion. He's mine, so why are they together? It's not proper for him to be alone with a mermaid. He embraces her and pulls her into a lingering kiss. My heart moves up into my throat as the passion heats between them.

"What are you doing?" I demand.

They jolt apart, both looking away. "I'm sorry, Maris. You weren't supposed to find out like this," Pasha says in a high-pitched voice. The guilt of her actions is written all over her face.

"What is it?" I ask, needing her to clarify.

Pasha tries to answer, but Ryn cuts her off. "We're just fooling around, Princess."

Pasha's face instantly drops into a scowl. I think there's more to their relationship than a few kisses.

"How could you?" Pasha says with a shaking voice. A tear falls down her cheek.

"I'm the victim here," I say, although I'm more shocked than angry.

"Poor Maris... Poor Maris. You're a princess and get to marry the most beautiful mer in the sea." Her tone is cruel, but I can also hear a hint of sadness.

"I'm not going to marry him now," I say, unable to hide how insulted I feel. And why is she trying to make me out to be the bad guy?

"I'll stop seeing her. You're the one I want," Ryn says, moving away from Pasha and a little closer to me.

"Yesterday, you couldn't get away from me fast enough. Were you together all night?" I think back to them disappearing about the same time. I feel like a fool for not seeing the signs. When I think about it, they've both been acting strangely for a while.

"I'm sorry," Ryn says, scratching his neck.

"You should be ashamed of yourselves, both of you." I don't wait for them to answer before getting away from the toxicity. The pain I should be feeling never comes, but the anger makes my tail curl. I rush to my father to tell him what's happened. He's out in the statue garden when I arrive.

"Father," I say when I approach.

"What's the matter? Why are you in yesterday's shells? Have you been to bed?"

"I've been out to a shipwreck. I saw Ryn and Pasha kissing." As soon as the words are out of my mouth, I realise I've made a mistake.

My dad's face turns an angry shade of purple. "What shipwreck? Do you know how dangerous those places can be? What if a lifeboat had found you? I forbid you from leaving the city. What were you thinking?" he shouts.

If I wasn't so worked up, I wouldn't have revealed my secret, but I don't correct his assumption about it being a new sunken ship.

"Did you hear me? The wedding's off," I sob. He's missing the point of my confession.

"We'll talk about this when you've calmed down."

I need him to understand I'm not backing down. "There's nothing to say." I cross my arms over my chest.

"Go to your room." He points towards my quarters. My dad's always been strict, but he's always listened to me.

"I'm not marrying him," I say, hoping he'll agree with me.

"You'll do as I tell you."

I bite down on my lip until it starts to sting. My anger turns to hurt as tears well up in my eyes. He's not considering my feelings. When my father told me I was to be mated with Ryn, I was crushing hard. I never thought I'd regret not having a choice. I turn my back to my dad and head towards my room. Instead of going inside, I do the one thing he told me not to. I leave the city in search of peace of mind.

SCORPIO
LIBRA
VIRGO
LEO

Chapter Two

AQUARIUS CONSTELLATION IS SEEN IN THE SEA REGION OF THE SKY

Maris

Thunder crackles loudly as lightning strikes across the midnight sky. It looks both beautiful and deadly. I can feel the warm tears run down my face to join the ocean. My bad mood has lasted all day, despite chasing sanctuary. Everything I thought was true is turning out to be a lie. My best friends are untrustworthy like my father said, and despite the fact Ryn is dating Pasha, it doesn't mean he won't be my husband. I could've dated other mermen, but I chose to wait for him. I've been taken for a fool and I'm not going to accept it. My father doesn't value my opinion, but I can change his mind. I won't be marrying a man who doesn't love me.

The sea is choppy as the storm whirls around me. The high waves and water spray fuel my anger. I can make my own ripples. A piece of driftwood hits my arm as it churns around. Another piece floats right past me as I see more pieces in the fore mist. It's a shipwreck, not random weathered branches from trees. If a boat has collided with some rocks, I'm guessing the human is still out there.

My daddy would tell me to let the gods have their fun, but as the unconscious body of a man comes into view, I find myself moving towards him. His thick blonde hair covers most of his face, and he seems to be unconscious. His skin is weathered in the way most sun walkers usually are. I'm not an expert on the species, but he doesn't look like the typical sailor. His hands aren't calloused enough, and he's kind of pretty for a man. He also doesn't have any waterproofs on or rubber shoes. The arm holding him above the water begins to lose its grip. I try to push him back on, but it's no use. If I don't intervene, he's going to sink. This is bad.

Swimming into Haiti's harbour is too risky when I can't hide under the water. I can't be seen to be rescuing a human or I'll be labelled a traitor. But I can't let him die when he's this close. Could fate have brought us together? Am I supposed to save him? There's a place I could take him until I can find a boat to carry him back to shore. It might be reckless, but I pull him onto my back before setting off towards the hidden caves. The entrance is underwater, but it's only for a short amount of time. I drag him under, barely missing his head on the top of the rocks. Once we're inside, I hoist his body onto the land. Holding myself up, I watch for his chest to rise. It's been longer than I think it should have been. I hit him hard in the solar plexus and water comes up through his mouth. He coughs as he gasps for air. Turning onto his side, the water falls to the ground. It's both gross and fascinating to watch. Once he seems okay, I start to leave.

"Wait," he says between coughs.

I hesitate. Saving a human is one thing, but letting him get close to me will be unforgivable. Hopefully, he'll think he's delusional from all the water he's ingested. "You'll be okay here. Rest up, and I'll find you a boat to take you back to land."

"What about the one I was in?" he asks.

I shrug. "I found you in the water."

"Are you a siren?"

"I saved you and this is the thanks I get," I say, shaking my head. I've had enough of people assuming things about me. Maybe my father was right about this, though. I should've left him be rather than give him stories to take home.

I lower myself into the water.

"Don't go. Please!" His tone seems desperate.

My hair becomes weightless as the air is traded for the water. I'm already a couple of meters down when doubt sets in. Should I have listened to him before I abandoned him? The ugliness waiting for me at home stops me in my tracks. The human already thinks I'm a creature of the sea. Would it be so bad to spend a little more time with him?

In less than ten minutes, I find myself resurfacing in the cave. The man's shivering from the cold water. "Why are you out in the storm?" I ask.

"I missed the weather forecast," he says, pulling his arms tightly around his chest.

"Is that some kind of oracle?"

"I guess, in a funny kind of way, it is. Do you have fortune-tellers down here?"

"We don't need to predict the weather on land."

"That's not what I meant." He blinked a few times, then rubbed his eyes. "Sorry, even seeing you with my own two eyes, I never thought it was possible to meet a mermaid. I mean, I hoped they were real, but wow. Do you believe in prophecies or signs from the gods?"

I never expected to meet a human, but also, I didn't

think he'd be questioning me on my beliefs. What a strange species. "Why do you want to know these things?"

"I'm curious, that's all. I've never met a mermaid before."

"You need to forget this ever happened. Once the storm starts to calm, I'll get you back to land. I think we should try to find a way to warm you up for now." His teeth are chattering and his skin's a strange colour.

"Do you have anything to start a fire?"

I frown. "It's not something we need to know how to do." I've seen campfires on the beach and read about them in books. My father's going to kill me if he ever finds out what I'm about to do.

I pull myself up onto the land. He watches me but makes no effort to move. I flip my tail so I can drag myself towards him. We hold our gaze, and I lean in to touch his lips with mine. Heat ignites as I deepen the kiss. This wasn't how I expected this to go. It feels nice to be close to him.

The pink tone returns to his skin, and using the essence I'm empowered with from the sea, he stops shaking. I've warmed him by giving him a gift from the ocean.

"Wow, that was some kiss," he says, looking as

shocked as I feel. I've never felt a spark like that before. "I'm Kasper. And you are...?"

I blink a few times, trying to clear my head. "My name isn't important." If it gets back to my father that some mad man is talking about a mermaid he met called Maris, I'm not sure he'd believe it wasn't my fault.

"Your tail is beautiful, and your eyes are as blue as the ocean." He softly strokes my hair. I watch his movement, confused by what's going on.

"What are you doing?" I ask, narrowing my eyes.

"You kissed me. A little flirting is harmless." He smiles so brightly I have to fight the urge to kiss his soft lips again.

I frown, shutting out my inappropriate thoughts. I'm a mermaid and he's a human. That's not a compatible match. "The kiss was to help you. I gave you help from the sea."

He studies me for a few seconds while leaning back on his hands. "Thank you. Okay, I can tell you're not like the girls from the hotels, so I'm going to cut the bullshit. I need to find the jug of Aquarius." He switches off the charm and turns deadly serious.

What girls from a hotel? Why am I being compared to humans? "And why would you think I could help with that? Everyone knows the zodiac sign is an air symbol." His over-friendly exterior is gone, and I guess mine is too. Where has being nice gotten me so far? My best friend betrayed me and my father doesn't trust my judgement.

"The lost city of Atlantis is underwater, and I think that's where the jug is hiding."

"You have a vivid imagination."

Kasper must fancy himself a treasure hunter, but nobody has discovered the city in five hundred years. I've heard about the legend of Aquarius. The water bearer's jug is said to heal life. In the wrong hands, the god's power could be used for evil. I don't know where the item is, and even if I did, I wouldn't show a human.

"Until this evening, I wasn't sure mermaids exist, but here you are. I have to believe the city is real and there is such magic."

"Why?"

He runs his palm over his hair, pulling the wet strands off his forehead. "Because I need to save him. I need to save my brother."

The desperation in his eyes is enough to make me consider helping him, but Daddy raised me better than to fall for that. It's one thing to save his life but another to heal a sick human. I move back towards the water. "I can't help you."

"Please. I'm begging you." He grabs my arm.

I shake him off. "I'm sorry. I can't."

Resurfacing was a mistake. Maybe saving him was a bad idea also. I plunge back into the depth of the sea and get far away from the human that's messing with my mind. They say mermaids can steer people towards their death, but that human may just be the death of me.

SCORPIO
LIBRA
VIRGO
LEO

Chapter Three

Aquarius is identified as 'The Great One' in Babylonian stars

Pasha

I turn over, hating myself for being weak. Ryn shouldn't have this much control over me. It's obvious I'll never be his first choice of bride, and I should stop putting up with his scraps of attention.

I slither from the bed and gaze out of the window. Atlantis is quiet at this time of night. The only sounds come from the few bubbles of air escaping from the clam statue. The view from the royal quarters is nothing like the tiny grain of light I have in my small cave. I gaze over at Ryn sleeping peacefully and wish I'd said no to coming here.

Instead of disturbing Ryn, I make a quiet exit. The staff entrance is the one I'm most familiar with, and I let myself out of the back door. Ryn cares for me, I'm sure of it, but I can't be his mistress for the rest of my life. I need to get away from him and try to keep the distance between us.

Out in the open, there's nobody around as I make my way home. Once I'm in the shadows, I see Maris. Usually, I'd avoid her when returning from Ryn's bed, but I need her to understand I never meant to hurt her.

"Maris," I say as loud as I dare.

"Pasha?" she asks, sounding startled. "I didn't expect to see anyone." She clutches her chest like she's spooked.

"I need to talk to you."

"There's nothing to be said. You've been seeing my future husband behind my back and my father still wants me to marry him."

"I'm sorry, Maris. I tried to tell you about my relationship with Ryn." My efforts probably haven't been good enough because I was scared of what she'd think. I dip my head in shame.

"And my father tried to warn me about you." Her tone is bitter, and I probably deserve it, but we've been friends for a long time. I wish she understood. It was a mistake to let him kiss me at graduation, and when I went to talk to him the day after, I shouldn't have let it happen again. The guilt has been eating me up inside, and hearing him say we meant nothing hurt. I really like Ryn, and I thought he felt the same way. I never meant to cause Maris pain, especially when my relationship was based on lust. I'm such a fool for letting this get out of hand.

"That hurts. We're friends." I reach out to her, but the coldness in her eyes makes me stop.

"You're nothing to me."

My chest aches as her words cut deep. I hate how she's looking at me, and it's my fault. I want her forgiveness. Tears cloud my vision. "Please."

She turns her back on me.

I'm a terrible person. But is it so wrong that I wanted to feel happy just for a little while? I nod to myself when she doesn't answer and slowly start to leave. When I glance back, she's gone. Hopefully, if I give her more time, she'll forgive me. Although, I'm not sure what I can say that will make this right between us.

Sadness washes over me as I reach my cave. It's small, cramped, and on the outskirts of the city. I wish this wasn't where I belonged, but it's getting harder and harder to believe I can be anything more than this.

"Where have you been?" my mother asks as I enter.

"Hello. I was visiting a friend," I say, trying to keep the mood light.

"You need to get your head out of the coral and into the factory where you belong."

"I still have one more week before I have to sign up."

"Don't do this to yourself, Pasha." She tries to comfort me, but I move away. The events committee might still offer me a job. I can't give up the tiny glimmer of hope I have yet. My mother and two of my sisters all work at the shell factory, but I want more.

"Did you just accept your fate?" I ask her.

She bites her lip, looking off into the distance. "My story is complicated. I love you and your sisters, but I've spent most of my life scraping by. You need to find a good job and a hardworking husband. Don't make the mistakes I did."

"I'm not going to get pregnant." My mum gave birth to my sister before her eighteenth birthday, and my dad left when I was young.

"You're also not going to find a good man if you keep fraternising with the royal." It's an unspoken rule a royal will marry someone of the same status. I'm part of the working class, so I should find a similar merman. If I got a job in the king's quarters, it would open up my options to those mer too, but not someone like Ryn.

I think back to graduation and the way he was

looking at me. He told me I was special, but in reality, I was a fool for trusting him. Unlike Maris, my career is my focus, not finding a mate. A tug of guilt fills my chest. Maris is in love with the idea of being in love but I shouldn't have been the one to burst her bubble.

My mother's right. I need to forget about Ryn and Maris so I can focus on my future like I should've been doing all along. It's hard to accept this is the most I can be, but I need to stop dreaming. "Just give me my last week."

She nods. "Don't be late on your first day. I'll bring the paperwork home tomorrow."

I fight back a tear. "Sure."

I swim into bed with my sisters. This is where I belong. I can help my mother with the bills and I can find a suitable partner. I'm going to accept my fate, but first, I have to fix what I've broken.

Ryn

"I saw Pasha sneaking out of your room this morning," my sister says.

"Leave it, Nerida," I say, annoyed she's bringing this

up. It's not the first time she's seen her and it won't be the last.

"You have the chance to be king. Don't fuck it up by sleeping around."

She's only thinking of herself and how many suitors it will open up for her if I marry our leader's daughter. "Don't pretend that you care."

"If you didn't think with your dick, I wouldn't have to."

Maris is a sweet girl and not the type to fool around. She's also too naïve. There's more to life than getting married and bringing up a family. I couldn't wait for Maris, especially when she might not satisfy my sexual cravings. Pasha is curvier and has darker features. She's also headstrong and adventurous. She's beautiful in a way I've never seen before. It's unfortunate Maris found out about my rendezvous with Pasha, but she won't hate me forever. From the way Maris looks at me, I can tell she worships the ground I walk on. Once she understands it was a mistake to get involved with someone else, she'll come around. "Go find your own toy and leave me alone," I say.

"If you speak to Maris, I'll give you some peace." Irritation washes over me. Nerida must've been listening to Pasha and me arguing.

"You know her father won't let me anywhere near

her." It's improper for me to talk to Maris alone, which is also part of the problem. It's hard to get to know someone who is always surrounded by other merfolk.

"It's a good thing I saw her heading over to the coral reef, then."

Before she has a chance to taunt me further, I swim for the door. "You could've told me that right from the start."

"Nice chatting with you, brother," she says over her shoulder.

I brush my hands through my hair as I make my way up to the coral reef. Maris is always sneaking off. I've followed her a few times, but it's usually to do something boring like scouting the harbour for trapped animals.

At first, I think I've missed her. I'm about to turn back when she sinks out of a nearby cave.

"What were you thinking?" Pasha's voice rings loud.

"Why are you following me?" Maris asks.

"It's a good thing I was before you did something stupid." Her tone is scolding, which is unusual. She has no authority over Maris.

"Like you're an expert at making the right choices." Maris's words are just as fierce.

"At least I haven't smuggled a human."

The words hang between them and I can't stay quiet any longer.

"You've done what?" I burst out. Maris is usually the sensible one. Surely, she wouldn't do something so crazy.

"Great. I don't need either of you butting into my business."

"Where is this human?" I ask. First, I look at Maris, but when she doesn't answer, I turn to Pasha.

"Stay out of this, Ryn," she says.

"Is it up there?" I ask, pointing to the cave they both just came out of.

"He's called Kasper." Maris covers her mouth when she realises what she's just said.

She's been talking to this human. I don't wait for her to say anymore. Instead, I swim up into the cave and out of the water. The guy is standing, towering over my position.

"There's more of you?" he asks.

What a stupid question. "You do know how to reproduce?" I smirk. He's no match for me. I'm bigger, better, and more handsome.

"You must be the boyfriend, then?"

"Yes, of course I am," I spit.

"No, he's not," Maris fires back, shaking her head.

"We'll discuss this later. Once I've disposed of this human."

"You can't just kill him." Horror rings from her words.

"What were you planning on doing with him?" I narrow my eyes.

"He was going to drown. I had no choice but to save him." Maris waves her hands around like she's making perfect sense.

"Yes, you did." I thrust my arms out forcefully to exaggerate my opinion.

"We can't kill him," Pasha says, rubbing her head. She looks stressed as she loops around in a pacing manner.

"We can't let him return to the land. He'll bring more people to our waters," I say.

"Guys. Sorry to interrupt this crazy plan you're making up, but I have no intention of revealing your secret. All I want is the jug." Kasper points to a tattoo on his leg of the Aquarius water healer. In mer school, we learned a lot about stars and the zodiac system.

"I already told you, we don't have it," Maris says. Her voice is still shouty, but her words soften towards the end.

"What are we going to do?" Pasha asks. She drags her hands down her face.

I point at the picture. "Actually, I've seen this before." I shrug, not giving all my secrets away at once.

"If you paid attention at school, it was in the curriculum," Maris bites out.

She's obviously still pissed with me. It's not that I don't like her, but the sooner she realises the world isn't all sunshine and calm waves, the better. That's always been her problem. She's smart, pretty, and annoyingly good-natured. Although, this human might be her downfall.

"Close to Atlantis City, I've seen that exact picture." It'll be fun to liven things up around here. An adventure sounds good, especially if it helps Maris see the sense in her actions. She needs me by her side to rule the kingdom. I'm the right person to be king.

"Excellent. Then you can help me," Kasper says.

I never thought I'd agree with a human, but this is my opportunity to fix my relationship with both mermaids. I won't let him leave the ocean, but I can prolong his fate. "Okay."

"Wait. Why would you help him?" Pasha asks, narrowing her eyes.

I shrug. "I'm bored. I'll try anything to make my day more exciting."

She huffs and folds her arms. I guess she thinks that was a dig at her. "Is that all I am to you?"

I don't get a chance to answer because Maris cuts in. "If you're going, so am I."

I rub my hands together. I'm glad Maris is willing to accept the challenge. Maybe I have her pegged all wrong.

"I guess I'm in too," Pasha says in defeat. She turns her back on me.

Having two women pissed at me is going to make this interesting. I only need one mermaid to forgive me, and it's not Pasha.

SCORPIO
LIBRA
VIRGO
LEO

Chapter Four

The Aquarius constellation has three meteor showers

Maris

This seems like the start of a bad joke. My ex-best friend and ex-to-be are helping a human. They agreed to assist him so easily I doubt their motives are sincere. I feel protective of Kasper, and I can't let them kill him.

"Maris, can I talk to you?" Pasha asks.

I flinch at the sound of my name. This is all going wrong, and now Kasper knows my name. It probably would've come out eventually, but I'm losing control of this situation fast.

"I'm not ready to forgive you." I must be crazy for thinking I can get past the betrayal, but she's one of my oldest friends. She told me I didn't really know Ryn, and she was right, but maybe I don't know *her* as well as I think, either. I only saw what I wanted to.

I didn't realise she was following me when I entered the cave. As soon as her eyes caught sight of Kasper, she knew I'd saved him. Call it best friend intuition or whatever, but she knew. She didn't shun me for my actions. Instead, she wanted to help me get out of this mess I've created. My anger towards her is already weakening.

"Is life really that dull? What's the real reason you want to help a human?" I ask Ryn. Within a short space of time, I've realised I don't know this merman at all, and I want to understand him. What does Pasha offer him that I didn't, and why didn't he tell my father he wasn't interested in being set up with me? If I'd spent more time with him, would we have been compatible?

Pasha looks like she's going to interrupt but thinks better of it.

"Atlantis needs livening up. It can be a real drag at times." Ryn shrugs. "Besides, I want to make it up to you, Maris, and it seems like you want to help this human."

"You can be a real asshole sometimes," Pasha says to

Ryn, crossing her arms. Her eyes fill up like she's on the brink of tears, but she blinks them away. He seems to be good at hurting her feelings, and for some reason, she still likes him. It can't just be his good looks she's attracted to.

"So, it's agreed. I get the jug, and you can have whatever treasure we find?" Kasper asks, interrupting our tense moment.

"You'll keep our existence a secret?" I ask to make sure we're crystal clear about what I want.

He nods. "I don't mean you any harm. As I told you, my brother's unwell and I need him to drink from the jug. That's all."

"Okay," I say.

"Where did you find the symbol?" Kasper asks Ryn.

"Aren't you forgetting something? You can't breathe underwater. You should stay here and we'll report back." Ryn smiles like he's pleased with this plan.

"Can't Maris kiss me again and pass on her voodoo magic?" Kasper says.

My eyes widen. "I don't have voodoo magic."

"You kissed him!" Ryn barks, and Pasha laughs.

"Good for you," Pasha says, looking a little more cheerful.

"He was freezing to death. I had no choice." I throw

my hands up in the air. I catch them together, and they're the ones making a fuss over a kiss.

"You had multiple chances to let him die as nature intended, and you chose to save him. What's wrong with you?" Ryn asks in outrage.

"I can see trust is going to be a problem here," Kasper chips in. He's right, though. Trust seems to be my weakness. I should be more careful.

"When you catch your best friend and your betrothed together, I'd say there's definitely a trust issue here," I say. Pasha's mouth falls open as she loses the ability to speak. Ryn tries to give me another one of his hurtful answers, but I wave my hand to silence him. "I can make you a potion to breathe underwater and these two can find you some seaweed to cover up your legs while we're close to the city."

"I'll make the potion. You stay with the human," Pasha says and swims out of the cave. Ryn looks at us both but doesn't say a word as he leaves.

"I think you need to find some better friends," Kasper says.

"And look where that's got me," I say, pointing to him. Guilt immediately creeps in. "I'm sorry."

"It's okay. It seems you're having a bad day."

"More like two," I mutter.

"Thank you for saving my life and helping me."

"Sure." Deep down, I'm not sure why I'm doing these things. It goes against everything I've been told.

Kasper wades into the water, heading towards me. I didn't get a chance to have a good look at him yesterday. His body is like a painting covered in drawings. He has a mermaid tattooed across his muscly chest and my fingers itch to touch it. He makes the first contact by running his thumb along my breast shell, and I inhale a sharp breath. I could tell him he's overstepping the line, but I'm just as curious. Giving in to temptation, I allow myself the pleasure of exploring his skin. My hair has little starfish in it, and he touches each of them.

"You're beautiful." This isn't the first time he's complimented me, and he sounds sincere.

I glance up from his chest into his blue eyes. The fun and carefree attitude I see in Ryn isn't behind Kasper's eyes. His gaze is intense and full of stories. "Why were you out in the sea last night?"

"I've been searching for the jug."

"Without any real leads?"

"I was looking for Atlantis."

We continue to stare at each other.

"I've lived there my whole life and I haven't found the jug, so what was your plan? You haven't got diving equipment and your boat wasn't up to the task."

He's taken aback by my words and moves back.

“This is what a desperate man looks like.” He holds his arms out wide and slowly turns around.

He isn’t like anyone I’ve met before. The stars of Aquarius decorate his back, and I’m drawn to him. He makes my crush on Ryn seem unimportant, but he also makes me wary. I don’t want to get caught up in my head again, and I already know we don’t have a future together.

Ryn and Pasha return. They prepare Kasper for our journey, and even though there’s a strange vibe, we keep our conversation light-hearted. Once we’re ready, we set off for the location Ryn has in mind.

The place Ryn brought us to doesn’t look special. I’m not sure what I was expecting, but this isn’t it. “It’s just a rock,” I say.

“No. It’s a rock with a drawing on it,” Ryn replies.

Kasper doesn’t seem to be as deflated as I am. He studies the drawing and touches the rock.

“What’s he doing?” Pasha asks.

“I don’t know.” I shrug. “Human things.” I smile, and she smiles back. It’s hard to stay mad at her.

“Don’t you have a mermaid library or something?” Kasper asks.

"Sure we do. I'm not sure how big the zodiac section is, though," Ryn says.

"How did you find this relic?" Kasper asks. His lips turn down like he can't understand why Ryn's not more curious about his surroundings.

"How do you know it's not just a drawing some merkids did while messing around?" Pasha asks.

"I don't know mermaids, but I'm pretty sure a kid wouldn't draw a dude with a jug," Kasper says.

"There are sexier gods," Ryn chips in.

"Depending on the mythology reference, the water carrier might not have been a god."

"You're very knowledgeable on Aquarius," I say.

"I have to be if I want to be a successful treasure hunter."

"This isn't just about getting a prize, though, is it?" I've seen the desperation in his eyes, but I need to confirm what's in his heart.

"You know it's not." He looks deep into my eyes. It feels like we're connecting on another level. I can feel his pain and determination.

We continue to stare at each other with intensity. A beam of bright light shines down from the surface and touches the stone. It's unlike anything I've seen before. The Aquarius drawing shimmers like the water is flowing from the jug. We break our moment to look at what's happening.

A whirl of sand begins to move down, and a hole in the ground opens up. My mouth falls open, and I can't believe we've been close to this secret for so long, and now we have a chance to explore it.

LEO
VIRGO
LIBRA
SCORPIO

Chapter Five

AQUARIUS IS BEST SEEN IN AUTUMN IN THE NORTHERN HEMISPHERE

Kasper

The moment the ground rumbles and the cave starts to open up, my heart pounds in my chest and the spark of hope explodes into an overwhelming feeling. I could save my brother. I have to believe this will work. Now I have a lead, it really could happen.

The others are slow to react, but that's not my style. I'm the first to enter the secret cave, and I don't wait for them to join me. The beam of light we saw on the outside is split into tiny shimmers in here.

"Wow. It looks like stars," Maris says.

"What do you know about stars?" Ryn asks.

Maris narrows her eyes and I can feel the tension between them.

"Maris isn't the sweet, obedient flower you think she is. She's smart and adventurous. If you'd bothered to dig deeper, you'd have realised she's spent many nights exploring outside the city. Everyone has their guilty pleasures, including Maris," Pasha says.

"I like gazing at the stars," Maris says with a smile.

"I hate to break whatever this is up, but does anyone recognise any of these patterns?" I ask, moving closer to the wall. The holes are no bigger than fingerprints. I poke one of them but can't feel anything other than the water. If these were just gaps in the cave, wouldn't they fill with sand from the seabed?

I've been staring at the patterns for fifteen minutes before anyone speaks. "Do you think they could be linked to the zodiac signs like the jug?" Maris asks.

I smile. She's a smart woman. Using the new idea, I look back across the cave as if it was the night sky. "I could kiss you," I say.

"Hands off," Ryn says.

"What difference would it make to you? You've shown your true colours," Maris snaps, but there seems to be a wavering undertone of hurt.

"Whatever I say, I can't win. If I tell you I made a mistake, I'm an asshole, and if I say I had a connection with Pasha, I'm still the bad guy." Ryn shakes his head.

"Which is it?" Pasha crosses her arms over her chest.

They're both beautiful, but Ryn's an idiot. Any guy who dates two women has a death wish, especially if they're friends like these two appear to be.

Ryn runs his hands over his hair, clenching his fists tightly on the ends. He probably doesn't deserve it, but I'm willing to take some of the heat off him. It's not like I'm a saint myself. "Does anyone recognise any of the constellations?" I've seen pictures of Aquarius, but looking at everything all together is jumbling my memory.

"My birthday is February 14th, which makes me an Aquarius. From what I can remember, the stars resemble an E," Maris says.

I can't take my eyes off her. It's like fate brought her to me that night, even if she doesn't have all the answers. Everyone is on board with looking for the stars we need, but it's no use. We need more help.

"We should visit the library," Pasha suggests.

"And what if the cave closes? I don't want to risk it," I say.

"How about you and Ryn go search for a book, and

I'll stay here with Kasper." Maris nods like she's agreeing with her own plan.

"I don't think that's a good idea." Pasha shakes her head.

"Well, I'm not asking. I'm telling you to go. I think it would be in everyone's best interests for you two to clear the air." Maris points towards Ryn.

Pasha rubs her neck. "I want closure on our situation, but it's you I want to talk to."

"Have you seen each other before you discovered me with Kasper?" Maris's lips thin like this answer means everything.

"Yes, but..." Pasha starts.

Maris holds up her hands. "I don't want any more mixed messages from either of you. Talk it out so we can all move forward." Maris has an authority about her which makes me think she could be important.

Pasha considers arguing some more but struggles to convince Maris. "Okay, we'll go. Are you sure you'll be all right?"

"Yes, now go." Maris stands her ground and they do as she requested. Once we're alone, silence falls over us.

"Do you want to talk about it?" I finally ask.

"No. Do you want to talk about your brother?"

"No."

"Okay."

"Okay." This is where most girls I've dated would start to rant, but not Maris. Her thoughts stay in her head as I watch her study the cave. "The guy, Ryn... you should walk away from him."

She turns to look at me. "Don't worry, I will."

"And what about your friend. Is she a hussy?"

Her cheeks flame bright red. "I don't think that's her issue, but we haven't spoken about it. She's like family to me, and until now we've always looked out for each other."

"I don't care how good the orgasms he gave her were, he's not worth either of your time. Granted, your friend betrayed your trust too, but I think you should hear her out."

"Are you some kind of love expert?"

"No. I just know what it's like to carry regret around with you."

"Do you wish you'd spent more time with your brother?"

"I can't win. Every second with him is precious, but if I don't look for a cure, I'd be giving up. When this is all over, I hope I don't regret the moments we didn't share."

"Yeah. I understand what you're saying. You don't want to give up on hope, but it's taking you away from him."

"Exactly."

"Ryn was—or is—my intended. My father set up the match, and I was blinded by his good looks. My blinkers are firmly off now, though. He isn't the merman for me. I just need to convince my father."

"Is arranged marriage a thing with merfolk?" I'm curious about her culture and why her family would pick an unsuitable partner for her.

"It's not just about me. The bloodline needs to stay pure."

"What does that mean? Are some of you more human than others?"

"My blood is royal. They say we're closer to the gods. Plus, the person I marry will help me rule our people."

"Well, I'm honoured to have you helping a humble human. I have to ask, though... do they want you to marry a cousin of some form?"

"You might find that repulsive, but it's what my people have done for generations."

I hold my hands up high. "I've no grounds to judge anyone."

"Good, because I don't want you to treat me differently now you know I'm a princess."

"Okay." I smile at her. "You're just like the average mythical creature." She's so much more than the typical female. She's mesmerising.

Maris looks away. "This one?"

"Huh?" I ask.

"This star looks a little brighter than the others."

I shake my head. As I look at the place she means, I can see it. One hole has a slightly different shade of blue.

We move closer and feel around the rock. Our fingers touch as we move closer to the light. The beam penetrates farther into the cave. The Aquarius constellation stands out all on its own. We didn't need a book, although I'm not sure what we've done.

A door we didn't see before opens, and without hesitation, and we go through it. Once inside, the compartment seals, and there's no going back.

LEO
VIRGO
LIBRA
SCORPIO

Chapter Six

Spring is the best time to see the Aquarius stars in the southern hemisphere

Pasha

"Do we have time for a quick fuck before the library?" Ryn asks while we swim towards the main city.

Usually, this would send a tingle to my core, but not today. I scrunch up my face in distaste. My best friend needs our help and I can't let her down again.

"I don't think we should do that anymore." I shake my head.

He places his hands on my shoulders, making me stop swimming. "Come on, Pash. You know we're good together." He only seems to say the words I want to hear when we're alone. He has no respect for me and I need to put a stop to this.

"I said no."

His touch is soft and lingering. I can already feel myself melting into it. I shrug him off before I make a mistake.

Be strong, Pasha. "Let's get to the library so we can swim back to Maris."

"What's the hurry?" He tries to touch me again, but I move out of the way. With a forceful flex of my tail, I speed towards our destination, and he follows, matching my pace.

"We've left Maris with a stranger we know nothing about." I focus on the path in front of me rather than Ryn.

"He's weak in the water. She can handle him for an hour or two."

I narrow my eyes. Kasper seems genuine, and I wouldn't have left Maris if I thought he would mistreat her. That doesn't stop me wanting to check on her, though. It's worrying that Ryn would leave her with someone who he felt might need *handling*. "I have confidence in Maris's judgement if she wants to stay with Kasper. I'm happy to do my bit and help in any way I can."

He stops again, making me turn to face him. "You can't be serious. We shouldn't let him go."

"He already told us he's only interested in the jug."

"And you believe him?" He scowls.

"Yes, I do." Kasper seemed desperate. I don't know the full details of how Maris found him, but she wouldn't approach a land creature for no reason.

"He's a human. We shouldn't be helping him, and we certainly shouldn't be letting him return to land. He's a threat to us all."

"If you feel this way, why are you helping?"

"For Maris." An involuntary frown creeps onto my face, but I try to recover quickly. It hurts that he chose her over me. "And for you," he adds, but it's too late. My priority is Maris and our friendship. I need to forget my feelings for Ryn so I can repair the damage they've caused. If I'm going to gain her trust again, I have to focus on her, not Ryn.

"Let's get the book and get back to them." I turn, batting away tears. Just because I'm choosing Maris, that doesn't make this easy. Once my heartbeat steadies, I can think a little more clearly.

"Do you have a library card?" Ryn asks.

"No." When I left home, I never imagined I'd be visiting the library.

"Then let's stop by my place. We can grab the card after we make up."

He never gives up, but I have to break the pattern. Until now, I hadn't noticed his resilience in getting his own way. "I don't think so."

"Then what's the plan? You never allow me to see your home."

I've always been embarrassed by my family's tiny cave, and I didn't want the divide between us to be so obvious. Now it doesn't seem so important, but I don't want my mother questioning our relationship.

"I'm not taking you there," I tell him.

"Then what? Are you going to steal the book?"

I blink a few times. "That's crazy talk. You can go and retrieve your library card while I wait outside."

"You're becoming a bore, baby."

"Don't be an asshole."

"Fine." He crosses his arms.

We reach the square fountain, which is near the royal quarters, and I take a seat while Ryn goes to his room. Fish, mermaids, and mermen pass as they go about their day. I watch some of their interactions, wondering where I'll fit. Once I start working at the factory, moments of freedom will be rare.

I'm lost in thought when someone comes to stand in front of me. "Have you seen Maris?" Adella asks.

She's one of the royals and has always looked down on me.

"No. Why? Is there a problem?" I'm guessing she hasn't told anyone where she is and I'm not going to give away her secrets.

"The king is worried. She hasn't been seen since last night."

"I saw her passing through the square this morning," I say, knowing I can't be the only one.

"Did she say where she was going?"

I shake my head.

"If you see her, tell her to come home."

I nod. My web of untruths is deeply woven. There's no point trying to untangle them now.

She leaves to ask more merpeople about Maris, and I listen to the echoes of her disappearance. Maris is adventurous, and her father is overprotective, but she always comes back. Even if she wasn't with a human, I would've kept her secret. I've made mistakes with Ryn, but I care about my friend.

"We need to get out of here," Ryn says when he returns.

"I saw Adella. The king is looking for Maris." I bite my nail.

"Yes. I've just been asked by a few members of my family."

"What did you say?"

"What do you think?" His lips thin like he's unimpressed I'm questioning his loyalty.

"I need to be sure you haven't said anything."

"And be caught as an accomplice to snuggling a human into our world? I don't think so."

I smile, satisfied the core of his answer is self-centred. It reassures me he isn't lying.

"Come on." I gesture towards the way we need to go.

We make it to the library after being asked another three times where Maris is. My stomach feels uneasy. She never goes out for long, and I'll be glad when she's home.

There's a full shelf of books on astrology, and we sit looking through the books. "As long as it has a picture of Aquarius, does it matter which book we pick?" Ryn asks.

I shrug. We can't take them all and I have no idea what else we might need to know. "I think we should take the zodiac atlas and the book all about Aquarius."

"Okay." He takes the books to the desk and checks them out. We swim back to Maris and Kasper's location without any difficulties.

"Maris, we're here," I say as we enter the cave, but she's nowhere to be seen.

She and the human are missing. Thoughts of her being kidnapped flash through my mind. I try to settle the sickly feeling in my stomach. They might be looking for more clues, or maybe they solved this one.

"Pass me the atlas," I say, taking it from under his arm. I flick to the map of the sky I need and study the stars. Ryn stands over my shoulder, watching me match up the holes in the cave. "There," I say, touching the wall.

"What now?"

"I don't know. See if there's a button or something."

We spend almost an hour trying to solve the secrets of the cave, but it's no use. If Maris solved this riddle, she did better than us. I just hope wherever she is, she's safe. I lie on the seabed, feeling defeated.

"Do you think we should tell the king Maris is missing?" Ryn asks.

"No. We'll give her some time and see if she shows up."

"Okay. We'll do this your way. I'm not waiting here, but come find me when she gets back."

He leaves me to consider my options. A couple of hours later, I'm still no closer to finding Maris or understanding the cave. I don't want to stay here all night, so I head home. The feeling in my stomach doesn't settle, and I vow to return to the cave tomorrow.

SCORPIO
LIBRA
VIRGO
LEO

Chapter Seven

Fourteen of Aquarius's stars have planets

Maris

"Why does it have to be so dark in here?" I ask. We've been swimming in tunnels for longer than I'd like. For all I know, we're going round in circles.

"Can you use your magic and light a spark?" Kasper asks.

I can barely see his face, but I sense his playful smile. If I could make a light, I would've done it instead of freaking out when the door shut behind us.

"I don't have any magic." I laugh.

"You saved my life, made me feel warm, and gave me the ability to breathe underwater. A small spark should be easy."

"Those are just some of the things mermaids can do. It's nothing special." I shrug, although he can't see it.

"A human can't do those things."

"Have you ever tried? How do you heal sick animals and plants?"

"We take them to the doctor." He sounds so serious all of a sudden.

"Like an oracle?"

"No, like a scientist. They can use herbs for medicine, but it isn't magic. It's tested and proven to work." All the playfulness is gone, and I wonder if his thoughts have turned sad.

"That sounds like an oracle to me."

"I guess it probably does, but doctors don't make future predictions unless it's because you're a ticking time bomb."

"Is that what your brother is? I'm sorry, that was insensitive." Death isn't a doorstep I've set foot on in a long time. My mother died when I was three, and I don't remember it well. My memories of her are like dreams.

"It's okay. My brother has cancer. It's not something that can be cured. Are you mortal?"

I'm relieved he's comfortable enough to keep the conversation rolling. "Yes. Mermaids don't live forever. We also don't have the magic to heal your brother."

"Unless we find the jug."

"Yes. Finding the jug in the sea would prove me wrong."

"What made you want to help me?"

He's been real with me, and I want to return the favour. "To be honest, I've been having a rough few days and needed a way to take my mind off things." It's only part of the truth, but it's the only bit I'm willing to admit.

"Is this to do with Ryn?"

"A little." I'm so over my crush on him.

"So, tell me what's going on."

"I thought we weren't doing that." I'm only just coming to terms with the fact I can't be who everyone wants me to be and be happy.

"I shared, so now it's your turn."

"Fine. I guess I could use an outside observer. My dad's the ruler of Atlantis, and someday, the weight of leading will be on my shoulders. I've tried to be the kind of daughter he wants me to be, but sometimes it's hard. I don't want to marry a guy who doesn't love me, and I don't want to be the perfect example for everyone all the time. I want to be free to make mistakes and have some fun." I feel relieved at getting that off my chest. It's not that I want to make a mockery of my dad's rules, but it would be nice to be able to make my own decisions some of the time.

"You should do it. Take some time off from being a princess and live a little."

"My dad's probably already going crazy. He sent me to my room after I told him I wasn't going to marry Ryn."

"You sneaked out?"

"Yes."

"You rebel." The playfulness is back in his voice.

I push his shoulder. "I've slipped out before."

"Okay, but I bet you've never spent time with a human before."

"You have me there." I hold up my hands.

"What's the punishment for helping someone like me?"

I cringe. "Death."

"That's extreme." He laughs, but it sounds unnatural.

"Not mine." Oh, God. I just made it worse.

"Gulp. Let's hope your boyfriend doesn't turn me in."

I laugh. There's a weird, dark-humoured vibe

between us, but it almost feels like we're flirting. "He's not my anything anymore."

"Does he know that?"

"I'm not sure what Ryn thinks. When I spoke to my father, it seemed I might be the one who's wrong. He still wants us to be matched, but I'm going to stand my ground. I don't want a relationship with him. Everyone else will have to accept it."

"Good for you."

I like his praise. It's like I've done something great, even though I haven't given the message to the right people. I never realised I needed someone in my corner. "Thanks."

"But first, I'm going to give you the adventure you deserve before you have to become a queen."

I smile. Even if this journey only takes a day, I'm happy to go on it. "I'm looking forward to it."

For the first time since we entered the passages, there's an opening into a bigger space. The darkness is lifted by blue light, and I can finally see Kasper's features. His chiselled jaw and kind eyes are nice to look at. He feels along the walls as I follow him. "Are you ready?" he asks.

"For what?"

He pulls hard on a lever and a door opens. The burst

of light makes us shade our eyes. “Blue obsidian will set you free,” I read from the wall once we’re inside the room.

“It’s the handle,” Kasper says, holding up a piece of clay.

“And where is the rest of it?”

“My guess is we need to find a volcano with blue obsidian.”

“On land?” I ask.

“Unless you know of any underwater volcanoes, I think the next piece is on land. Can you leave the water?”

“How do you know it’s in more than two bits? Maybe the handle just fell off.”

“Because the diagram next to where I found this part suggests we’re looking for five pieces to make the whole jug. Stop avoiding my question. You said you want adventure and to help me, so will you follow me into my territory, or are you scared?”

“I can shed my tail for a while, but I’ve never done it.”

“Why not?”

If I admit it’s because I don’t leave the sea because it's forbidden, he’ll know my disobedience is mild.

“This is my home. I’ve never wanted to leave.”

“What about now? Will you come with me, Maris?”

Butterflies flutter in my stomach. I should want the things Kasper is offering me. This might be my only chance to do something so crazy, and I don't want to live with regret. If I go with him, I'll know I've lived my life to the fullest.

"Yes. I'll go with you. I'm trusting you to keep me safe."

"Always." We look into each other's eyes, but it feels deeper than that.

The way out of the cave opens up on its own, and Pasha is waiting outside for us. "Where's Ryn?" I ask.

"Thank the gods you're okay," Pasha says, hugging me. "The kingdom is looking for you. Ryn went back to try and take off some of the heat. We need to go home."

"Actually, I'm going with Kasper." He's standing behind me, but I don't look at his reaction.

We break apart. "You can't be serious."

"Cover for me?" I plead.

She rubs her head. "I wouldn't even know how."

"You owe me, so I know you'll come up with something."

She hesitantly nods. "Okay." She points to the books she's found. "Take these with you." Then she points at Kasper. "You'd better look after my girl."

"Yes, ma'am," he replies, and just like that, I'm

heading for the surface with a complete stranger, in search of adventure. I shouldn't have trusted Ryn, but now all my faith is in another man. I hope I've made the right choice.

LEO
VIRGO
LIBRA
SCORPIO

Chapter Eight

AQUARIANS WANT TO MAKE THE WORLD A BETTER PLACE

Kasper

Unwrapping the seaweed from around my legs, I place it around Maris. Her legs are the most beautiful I've ever seen. My attraction to her is like nothing I've felt before. Her flawless body is pretty from head to toe, and her heart seems pure, unlike the women I've been hanging out with lately. Trusting her came easily, which is unlike me.

Once she's dressed in her seaweed skirt, I lead her through the streets of Haiti. Her outfit doesn't raise any eyebrows because she looks like she's going to a party. I pick a flower from a flowerbed and tuck it into her hair. "Perfect," I say, and she smiles.

The hotels and houses closest to the beach belong to the rich. Maris is mesmerised by the buildings, and I hold her hand as we walk through the streets. I love watching her curiosity, and it doesn't fade as we move away from the prettier side of the island.

I hold her closer as the paths become narrow. "Watch your step."

"Where are we going?"

"To my home." It's too late to start searching the volcanoes. Besides, I'd like to study Lara's island guide before we set off.

She nods. "Will your brother be there?"

"Yes."

"It will be nice to meet him." She seems genuinely happy, and I can't control the feeling it gives me.

"Owen's going to love you."

"Will you tell him I'm from the sea?" A worry line wrinkles her forehead.

"Only if you want me to." I reassure her by caressing the back of her hand.

"Let me be the one to decide."

"Sure. We're almost here." I guide her over the uneven wood outside our house and open the door. My brother is on the floor when we get inside, and I rush over to him. With Maris's help, I get him back into his chair.

"What happened?" Owen asks.

"I'm sorry for leaving you. You must've fallen." Pain laces my words. He's getting worse, and I'm so close to achieving my goal.

"You've never brought a girl home. Who's this?" he asks, looking behind him.

"This is Maris. She's helping me. Are you okay?"

"Yes, I'm fine. What were you thinking? She knows where we live now." Usually, I wouldn't bring anyone here, but Maris isn't just 'anyone', and she isn't going to tell anyone where we live. He seems to have jumped to the wrong conclusion, and he probably thinks she's someone I'm dating that might eventually go to the police because I've stolen something. I can't blame him, really. That is usually why I'd be with a pretty lady.

"Maris isn't like the girls from the hotel. She's a treasure hunter like me."

"What if she's only after the prize?"

"Chill, brother. She's only here to help."

"From what we've discovered in Haiti, it's hard to believe someone would help without wanting something in return."

"Isn't my word enough?"

"Do you know what they'd do to you in jail?"

"You don't have to worry about me," Maris says.

"And why's that?" Owen asks in an almost hostile way.

"Because the land has nothing to offer me. I'm only here for a short visit, and I can't take anything back with me."

"Why not?"

"I have an overprotective father who wouldn't take kindly to me taking foreign objects back. I needed to get away for a while, but when I go home, my life will go back to normal."

"And where does your father think you are?"

"He doesn't know where I am. He's probably worried about me, but I won't stay long."

"Great. So your offences have upgraded from theft to kidnapping," Owen barks.

"She's here of her own free will."

"This is going to end in disaster."

"No. This might be the first big break we've had since arriving in Haiti."

"What do you mean?" His voice is a little calmer now.

"I'm trying my best to help you, but I need you to have faith. Stop second guessing my decisions. Everything I do is for you. It's for us." I rub my hand over my face.

"I'm sorry. I know you're trying to help, I just wish it didn't mean you had to sacrifice your morals."

"You're all that matters. Don't worry about me."

"Tell me about this change in luck?"

I pull out the handle of the jug. "Maris helped me find the first piece of the Aquarius jug." His jaw drops open, and I can't control the tears that run down my face. "We're going to save you." We hug, and I feel my brother's tears fall too. When we break apart, I rub my face, trying to pull myself together. Turning to Maris, I say, "Are you hungry? We should eat something. We don't know how long it'll take us to find blue obsidian, and we need to reenergize."

"Okay. What fish do you have?"

"Usually I'd have something in, but almost drowning dwindled my supply from the sea."

"What happened?" Owen asks.

"I got caught out in the storm and Maris saved me." I don't want him to worry, so I try to play it down as much as I can.

"I'm grateful for that." He touches Maris's arm.

"You can trust me, Owen. I'm not a threat to you."

He kisses her hand, and I think seeing the handle of the jug has gone to his head. Seeing them get along gives me a strange feeling. I don't want anyone to touch her. I'm glad my brother's warming to her, even if it's bringing out my possessive side.

"You two sit and talk while I see what I can whip up."

I can hear them deep in conversation while I fry some chicken.

Once I have three plates balanced on my arm, I make my way back to them. "How's it going in here?"

"I've been missing out. Your brother's a blast."

"He has the Colombo charm." Jealousy washes over me, but I shake it off. I drop a plate in front of each of them and take a seat.

"Are you a local to Haiti?"

"Pretty close, yes. I visit the docks all the time."

"You do?" I ask in disbelief.

"As often as I dare. There's something beautiful about the place where the land meets the water."

"I never thought of it like that before. It's usually the water I look at." When you have gorgeous views in the distance, it's easy to forget what's right under your nose.

My brother looks at her like she's a spectacular creature. "That's how I feel about sunsets. The place the sun disappears behind the sea is magical." He takes a bite of his chicken, and Maris copies him.

"Is it good?" I ask.

"Different. It's tasty." She looks at the food before eating another piece.

"Try the sauce. I made it myself," Owen says, adding some homemade tomato ketchup to Maris's plate.

She dips the chicken in and makes a yummy noise as she eats it. "Wow. You're a talented botanist."

"Unfortunately, I can't take credit for growing the tomatoes. Back home, I used to have a garden, but not here." He smiles sadly.

"Where's home?" Maris asks.

"England."

She seems to be trying to place the location in her mind, so I add, "The North Sea."

"Aw. It's a little cold for me there."

"Us too," I say.

"Are you a fan of the ocean?" Owen asks.

"Very much so," Maris says once she's finished the food in her mouth.

"Maris is more than a fan. She's an expert."

"A marine biologist is a great job," he says, jumping to conclusions.

"Yes. It's pretty great to be involved in something you love."

We finish the food and Owen falls asleep in the chair. "What do you say to us sharing the bed?" I ask.

She hesitates, but then agrees. "Yes. That sounds like a plan."

"Don't worry, I'll be a perfect gentleman."

I give her a spare toothbrush and an oversized t-shirt. She settles into my bed, and I climb in next to her. There's only one bed in our small apartment in Haiti. Luckily, Owen often stays in the chair.

"Good night, Kasper." She snuggles into the pillow, and I turn out the light.

"Good night, princess. May your dreams be sweet."

SCORPIO
LIBRA
VIRGO

Chapter Nine

THE ANCIENT WORLD NEEDED AQUARIUS TO MAKE GREAT CITIES IN THE VISION OF CREATING BETTER THINGS

Maris

"We need to go further inland to Thomazeau," Kasper says.

I've never been away from the sea for any length of time, but last night, it called to me. Moving away from the coast doesn't sound appealing. "Maybe I should wait here with Owen," I say, rubbing my elbow.

"You've made it this far, Maris. Now you have to go all the way."

"You're adventurous and your curiosity is inspiring, but I'm not like you."

He laughs and I pout. "I want to see you live a little. I dare you."

I smile. "Okay. I'm in."

We say goodbye to Owen before getting a bus across the country. Kasper spends the journey explaining some human things to me. The heat away from the water is uncomfortable, and the road is anything but smooth, although apparently, it should be a flat surface. Kasper doesn't seem to notice the bumps or the hot air as he continues to explain transportation.

"This is our stop," Kasper says, pressing the bell I've seen others use to make the bus stop.

We fight our way to the front of the bus and get off. "I'm glad that's over."

"You might not be saying that after the hike we need to do."

"We're not quitters, remember."

"Okay. Let's do this." He pushes his rucksack up onto his shoulders and takes hold of my hand as we take off into the landscape.

"I thought a volcano would be hotter."

"One that's erupted or unstable would be, but this one's more like a big hill." He sighs heavily.

"What if we can't find any blue obsidian?" I bite my lip.

"We were lucky with the first piece of the jug because Ryn had seen the Aquarius drawing. I doubt the other bits will be as easy to locate."

"So, if this is the wrong place, we have others to visit?"

"I've been searching for this treasure since my brother's illness became terminal. I want to find it as fast as possible, but Rome wasn't built in a day."

"I don't know much about Rome, but I think I understand what you're saying. This is going to take time."

"I'm willing to walk over mountains and swim to the deepest depths for my brother."

"You're a wonderful person."

"If you knew some of the things I've done to get here, you wouldn't be saying that."

"You sound like Pasha. She often tells me I can't understand her struggles, but my life isn't all rainbows and sunsets. It's not as bad as your situation, though. I understand you're desperate to change Owen's fate."

"You're sweet." He smiles.

I shouldn't be irritated by his words, but I am. I'd like him to see me as more than a sweet girl. I'm almost nineteen and want to be seen as a headstrong woman. I want to be taken seriously, and I thought Kasper understood that.

My lips dip down into a frown. “Thanks.”

“You’re going to rule a city one day. That’s a lot of pressure, but at least you can live for today and enjoy your freedom.” He caresses the back of my hand, and I’m grateful for his words. He does seem to get me, and he’s right. I have time to enjoy these moments.

“Let’s stop and enjoy the view for a few minutes,” I say, gesturing to a rock, which I sit down on.

“How are your legs holding up?” He strokes my knee, and it feels good. I’ve never been a touchy-feely person or been friends with anyone who is, but I don’t mind his attention.

“Walking’s not as fun as swimming, but after a little rest, I’ll be ready to race you up the hill.”

“Oh yeah?” He raises his eyebrow.

“Unless you think I’ll beat you on my inexperienced legs.”

“I’m not worried at all. I’m wondering what I get for winning.”

“Like a prize?”

“Yes. Don’t you have competitions under the sea?”

“Sure we do, but it would be frowned upon to beat a princess, so people tend to avoid inviting me.”

"Don't worry, princess. My moral compass isn't that strong."

I laugh at his refreshing attitude. "What if I find you some pearls if you win, and you can find me something precious."

"I can't afford anything like that. I was thinking a dare or a gesture."

"A dare?"

"Like standing up to Ryn and telling him what you really think."

"He knows how I feel."

"I doubt that very much."

"Okay. If I win, I want you to show me something beautiful."

"I can do that. Do you need a head start?"

"Don't treat me like a princess. While I'm here, I'm just Maris."

"Okay, just Maris. Are you ready?" He arches his eyebrow in amusement.

"Yes." I race off, and Kasper's hot on my tail. Laughter echoes around us, but I don't look back. I want to be first to the top of the hill.

"Hey, wait up," Kasper says, and it isn't long before he's matching my pace.

I slow once we get close to the peak. "I was expecting

more. Don't get me wrong, the views are beautiful, but the pictures of volcanos I've seen were less green."

"I agree with you completely. I'm disappointed." He wraps his arm around my shoulders, giving me a squeeze.

"So, what now? Do we find a spade and start digging?"

"It would be so much easier if the Aquarius symbol was just here or marked off in a guidebook."

"If it wasn't hard, then it wouldn't come with a reward."

"Are you guys doing a treasure hunt or something? We never saw one of those in the brochure," a woman, roughly in her sixties, says. She must be used to walking because she has a lot of equipment with her. My own body feels wobbly like jelly, and I'm glad we've slowed down. "Sorry, how rude of me. I'm Janice, and this fine young man is my grandson."

A guy about my age turns around and smiles. He's wearing sunglasses so I can't see his eyes, but he doesn't seem as enthusiastic about making friends with us as his grandmother does. "Leave the poor souls alone, Grandma. They're probably on their honeymoon or something."

"We're just friends," I say.

"We thought it would be a fun way to explore Haiti by looking for the dude holding the jug," Kasper says with ease. He's slipped into a persona I don't recognise, but we need to be careful who we share information with.

"I haven't seen anything like that around here, but in Los Haitises National Park there are lots of star sign pictures carved into the rocks."

Kasper curses, and I try to cover it up with a question. "Where is the park?" I ask.

"In the Dominican Republic, dear."

"Is it far?"

Kasper sighs heavily. "It's a lot farther than the bus ride here."

"We're heading back there later today if you want a ride," Janice says.

"Grandmother," the guy curses.

"That would be lovely," Kasper says, turning on the charm.

"Sorry for troubling you, but we could really use the help," I say to the guy.

He removes his glasses to expose his dark brown eyes. "It's okay. You can sit with me and tell me all about how you ended up here."

Kasper scowls. "Mandy gets travel sick, so I'd better sit with her." He's not being friendly, but I also don't miss the lie. He doesn't want these people to know too much about us.

"Don't worry, I won't be sick on the journey. I can take a potion." I'm not travel sick, but I go along with his story.

"She means a tablet." He pulls me closer to his side.

"Excellent. I love an adventure," Janice says.

We take a slower walk back down to the base of the volcano. "We're going to take the ride, but we need to ditch these two as soon as we have the information we need," Kasper says.

"They seem friendly enough."

"Trust is a weakness."

SCORPIO
LIBRA
VIRGO

Chapter Ten

AQUARIANS WANT A BETTER FUTURE, WHICH CAN MAKE THEM REBELLIOUS

Pasha

"Pasha, get out here," my mum shouts.

I wipe the sleep from my eyes and secure my shells into place. "What is it?" I say as I leave the bedroom. As soon as I round the doorway, I stop dead in my tracks. "Your Majesty." I dip my head, but my mouth stays open. The king has never been to my house, and maybe not even this side of town. *Maris.* She must not have come home yet.

"You're my daughter's friend," he says with authority.

"Yes. Princess Maris is a dear friend," I say, keeping my eyes to the ground. To lie to a king would be treason, but what choice do I have? I have to hold my nerve.

"She didn't come home, and I need to know where she is." It isn't a question. He already thinks I know where she is.

I shake my head. "I'm sorry. I can't help you."

"You can and you will."

"She means no disrespect, Your Majesty," my mother says. "Pasha, tell the king what he wants to know and stop playing games." Her tone is demanding.

I rub my forehead. "I don't have any information on Maris."

"Ryn!" the king shouts as Ryn enters my small home.

Fuck.

"Tell the king everything, Pasha. You owe it to the crown," Ryn says.

What did I ever see in him? His pretty face doesn't hide his ugly flaws. His words are a warning, and I have to take them seriously. Ryn wouldn't do anything to jeopardise his own future, so I doubt he's told the king everything he could have.

"I saw her early yesterday morning in the centre of the city," I say.

"What did she say to you?" the king asks.

"We'd had a disagreement. I tried to get her to forgive me, but she was in too much of a hurry."

Ryn gives me a pointed look and a sly smile ghosts his face.

"You brought me all this way to find out that?" the king says to Ryn.

"I'm sorry, Your Majesty. I thought she'd know more." He bows to the king.

"The two of you upset my daughter. You will find her and bring her home."

"We wouldn't know where to start," Ryn says.

"No more excuses. Neither of you will step foot inside Atlantis until she comes home."

"But..." I start.

My mum hugs me tight. "You can't banish them."

"I can and I will."

Like criminals, we're escorted by the royal guides to the edge of Atlantis. I say goodbye to my mother and the king wards the land. His words are binding, and we can't return home without Maris.

"I should've taken the job in the factory and stopped fooling around," I say, using my fin to kick a rock.

"If you'd admitted Maris had run off with a human, we wouldn't be in this mess."

"Me?" I look at him, balling my hand into a fist. "Why didn't you tell him the truth?"

"Because I want to be his son-in-law."

"Well, I respect my life enough to keep my mouth shut too."

And I want my friend back.

"So, what are we going to do?"

"The only thing we can." He shrugs like he doesn't know what I mean. "We have to go find Maris."

"We don't know whether she even made it out of the cave."

"I do. I didn't leave her there." I wave my arms in frustration.

"Then where is she?" he growls.

"She's gone in search of the jug." He would've known that if he hadn't returned home.

I don't tell him she's already found part of it. The interest he's taken in it tells me he wouldn't use it for the greater good.

"Do you know where she's looking?" He glares at me.

"No, but I'm pretty certain she's left the sea."

He grabs hold of my arm.

"Ouch! Get your hands off me." I pull away.

"Stop playing games and tell me how we're going to bring Maris home."

"She went with Kasper onto the island."

"What?" He goes to grab me again, but I swim back. "Why did you let her do that?"

"She's a grown woman. She can do what she likes." I fold my arms.

"That's my future wife. You should've stopped her."

My mind fills with negative emotions. It hurts that he still sees her as his future wife. I'm angry it takes something like this for him to acknowledge her as his betrothed and the way he's throwing it in my face because she's done something he doesn't like. It's like he forgets I have feelings, even if we weren't an official couple. I'm also annoyed he thinks anyone can stop Maris doing what she wants. She deserves a life partner who will respect her mind, and I deserve someone who puts me first. "She deserves better than you, and if she wants to explore the land with Kasper, who am I to say she can't go?"

"Come on, then." Ryn starts to swim away.

"You can't be serious. I'm not leaving the water." I follow him, despite my protest.

"Yes, you are. You heard what the king said."

I curse. "I've never been farther than the shipwreck."

"Today's your lucky day because you're going to go all the way." His tone oozes annoyance. He probably doesn't want to do this either.

"The last time I let you go all the way is how we ended up in this mess," I bite out.

He doesn't slow for me. It's like his mind is made up and he's ready for the mission.

We make our way to the harbour and Ryn helps himself to a few things from a docked boat. "Dry yourself off and put some clothes on from the lower deck."

"Have you done this before?" I look around, hoping we're not seen. I've never walked on my legs before, but he makes it look easy. He climbs on the boat, baring his ass. He uses a towel to cover up and offers me a hand.

"Not everything is black and white." I can't read his expression.

I have no idea what he means by that, but I doubt he's going to give me a better answer. I bite my lip before closing my eyes to concentrate on my legs. I wiggle my fin from side to side until each side feels like it's moving freely, and when I look down, my scales are gone.

My hand grips the side of the boat to steady myself, and I hoist myself up. Water flows over the deck while I fall to the floor. Once I've relaxed, I crawl towards the inner cabin. I hold the rail as I make my way down to the cabin. It feels strange to dry my skin. The long t-shirt I borrow from the boat looks like a dress I've seen in books. It wraps around my legs and feels restrictive. I don't know how anyone wears trousers, although Ryn slips them on with ease.

"Are you sure about this?" I ask.

"The shirt looks good, but are you wearing underwear?"

I pick up a tiny piece of material. "This?"

He nods and helps me into them, then he goes to exit the boat onto the land. I hesitate for a few seconds, but soon I'm standing on solid ground.

LEO
VIRGO
LIBRA
SCORPIO

Chapter Eleven

Aquarians are creative thinkers

Kasper

"I haven't had a Pop Tart in years," I say.

"They're easy when you're in a hurry. You can just pop and go," Janice says.

Her grandson, Colin, has pulled Maris away from me and towards the dining room table. After Janice found out we weren't married, she insisted on us having separate rooms. It took almost ten hours to get here yesterday, and it didn't make sense for us to turn down a comfy bed.

"Your eyes are like the deepest ocean," Colin says to Maris.

"That's because Mandy deserves to be beside the sea, soaking up the sun," I shout, so he knows I can hear him.

Once my breakfast is ready, I make my way into the dining room and take a seat. They both watch me as I bite into the Pop Tart, which is far too hot, but I try not to show it.

Janice brings a plate of food and sits in one of the other chairs. "Five minutes, everyone. I've booked a canoe for an hour's time."

"I'm a pastry chef back home. I would love to whip you up some fresh croissants," Colin says to Maris.

I look at Maris, hoping to get her attention, but she's blushing at Colin's attention. Irritation simmers under my skin. I've never been jealous before and I don't even know her that well.

"Come on. We're going to be late," Janice says, checking the clock.

"I haven't finished my coffee," Colin says.

"Put it in a flask. I made an easy breakfast so we could set off."

Janice drives us to Los Haitises National Park, and once we've arrived, I snag a guidebook from a departing tourist.

"What do you say to us taking two boats instead of one and having a race?" I suggest.

"That's hardly fair unless you're offering to pair up with my grandmother. She has forty years on Mandy," Colin says. Of course he'd want to ditch his own blood relative.

"I got the last canoe for hire, unfortunately. We'll have to enjoy each other's company instead," Janice says.

"It was so nice of you to do this for us," Maris replies.

"It's no problem," Colin says.

He didn't even do anything. His grandmother drove us, fed us, and gave us shelter. I bite my tongue. I don't want to cause a rift when I plan to jump overboard.

I scan the guidebook for information on Aquarius. What I'm looking for is less than half a page and only touches on the zodiac. The picture is of tiny gems embedded into a large rock. This doesn't look like it's going to be obvious, and depending on the location, we might have to come back after dark.

We climb into the canoe, and I take the seat in front of Colin. Maris settles in front of me, and Janice is in front of her. I lean forward, placing the guidebook on Maris's lap. She studies it before Janice takes it from her. "I know where it is, dear. You guys concentrate your strengths on getting this boat where it needs to be."

"Yes ma'am," I say.

"In time. Here we go," Janice says. The National Park ranger pushes our canoe away from the edge and we're off. "Dip and glide. Dip and glide."

"I'm pretty sure we need to be paddling at the same side. How did you guys manage without us?" I ask.

"Oh, we didn't come down the river. I got a guidebook, but Colin wouldn't bring me unless I found a few more people to share the rowing."

"Well, I feel used," I joke.

"My youth is escaping me. A little trickery is needed if I'm going to get what I want before I die."

"I'm glad you brought us," Maris says.

With a little help from Maris and the water, the canoe takes a steady journey down the river. I continue to paddle, although I can tell it's not needed. Neither Colin nor Janice question why it's suddenly become easy. For someone who says she doesn't have magic, Maris is exceptional.

"And what do you think of my grandson?"

The question brings me back to the present. I don't want her to have a thing with Colin, and Janice's hint wavers my confidence. Does she like him?

The back of Maris's neck turns bright red, and I dread her answer. "He's nice, but I'm not looking for someone."

I'm glad she didn't give a naïve response, and I'm even happier she shut it down. She may seem innocent at times, but she knows what she wants.

"Aw. Bad break-up?" Janice asks.

"My ex was also seeing my best friend."

"Tough times," Colin says.

"The guy's a douchebag," I point out.

"He must be an idiot to fool around on someone as gorgeous as Maris."

"She deserves the best fish the sea can conjure up." I'm already smiling when her shocked face turns around. I mouth, "Just go with it."

"Did you two ever have a thing?" Janice asks, waving at the two of us.

"She wishes," I say. A hard laugh rattles in the back of my throat, and the others join in.

"Seriously. Did you?" Colin asks.

"We've only known each other a few days," Maris admits.

"Then why are you doing this treasure hunt?"

"We were partnered together as part of a club we're in," I say.

"And what's the prize?"

"A year's worth of art classes," Maris lies, getting into the swing of how these mistruths work.

"You don't take me as the artist type, Kyle," Colin says.

"I'm a tortured soul." I keep my tone flat in the hope he'll drop it.

The river splits in two, and Janice indicates which way we should go. The web of lies about art and paint get thicker but come so easily.

"There," Maris says, pointing to the rocks. Her paddle slips into the water, and I lean over to grab it. The canoe drifts to the edge of the river, and I stand abruptly, ready to get off.

"This is my stop. It's been a pleasure." I quickly vacate the boat, pulling Maris along with me. We stand at the edge, waving.

"How will we paddle back?" Colin asks.

"Don't worry, I'll help," Maris says.

They try to reach the banking, but Maris keeps them on course.

"Telling them you'd help probably wasn't the best idea."

"You could've warned them we were leaving." She sounds a little annoyed, so I try to reassure her it was the right thing to do.

"It's better this way. We don't want anyone to follow us, especially with what's at stake."

"They know where we are."

"True, but it will take them too long to get back here. We had no choice but to escape. I don't trust Colin."

"You don't trust anyone."

"I trust Owen and... I trust you." I've never put faith in anyone as I have her. "What is it you saw?" I look around.

She points to an underwhelming collection of stones pushed into the rocks. None of them look like Aquarius. "According to the guidebook, this is the spot," Maris says.

I take a deep breath. "This was a colossal waste of time. We should've stayed in Haiti." I move away from the river, ready to trek back through the woodland.

"Kasper."

"What?" I say in a clipped tone. I'm so annoyed we're going to lose another day travelling. I turn around abruptly and she's standing too close. We're nose to nose. "What?" I lower my voice to a husky whisper.

"Are you jealous of Colin?"

"Why would you think that?" I've been trying to hide my feelings, but it seems I haven't done a good job of it.

"You've been acting weird since this morning."

"Fine. Yes. I'm jealous. Are you happy now?"

"Why would that make me happy?" She frowns, and her eyebrows wrinkle together.

"I'm not like one of your rich boys who are after your status." I probably shouldn't have said that, but Colin got under my skin.

"What does that even mean?"

"You can't play with me." We've moved so close I can feel her breath on my face.

"I wasn't." The chemistry between us is electric. A bright light appears behind Maris, and at first, I think it's an actual spark. We both turn towards the ultraviolet light.

"Aquarius."

"Blue obsidian."

We move closer to the glass-like structure. A small crack appears in the rock, and together, we prise it open to reveal the next piece of the jug. The inscription underneath it says, *Where land meets sea, the stars shine brightest.*

LEO
VIRGO
LIBRA
SCORPIO

Chapter Twelve

Aquarians Thrive on Knowledge

Ryn

Pasha strokes a kitty in the alley, while I ask another shopkeeper if they've seen Maris.

"What did you say was the name of the guy she's with?" asks one of the customers.

"Kasper. He's looking for a treasure map or something," I say, trying to be vague but giving enough information for it to be relatable.

"Are you sure it wasn't Kyle?"

"I think he said Kasper."

"A couple of nights ago, I went on a date with a guy called Kyle Columbo. He said he was a treasure hunter."

"There are probably lots of tourists trying to find a fortune in these parts," the shopkeeper says.

"What makes you say that?" I ask.

"It is rumoured the lost city of Atlantis is off these very shores."

The woman blows a raspberry. "Please. Give me a break. That's the same line Kyle tried to spin me right before he robbed me."

"What did this guy look like?" I ask.

"A beach bum. You know the type. Blonde shaggy hair and a long-lasting tan. He was talking about mermaids existing and needing to find treasure."

I cover my mouth to hide my expression. This could be Kasper, but I don't want her to know that. Even worse, we've left our princess with him. "Do you know where this guy lives or anything?"

"If I knew that, I'd be knocking down his door, not standing here waiting for my daddy to transfer me some money."

"It's done," the shopkeeper says, handing her some cash.

"Thanks." She turns to me, "If you catch up with Kyle or Kasper, whatever his name is, tell him to return my stuff before the police hunt him down."

"I'll make sure he knows people are looking for him."

I step back onto the street, ready to share the information with Pasha. She's sitting on the back of some guy's truck with the cat on her knee. They see me and wave. The guy bangs on the hood of the cab, and I start to run. He pulls Pasha farther onto the truck bed and the cat leaps off.

The truck speeds to life and they're getting away. I run as fast as I can, but I'm no competition for a machine. I'm breathing heavily by the time I finally give up. I hold my knees for support.

"Fuck," I shout, and a woman covers her kid's ears.

Maris is probably with a thief who steals jewels, and I'm not even sure what trouble Pasha's got herself into. I didn't want to do this but I have no choice but to go to my source on land.

Isaac knows my secret about being a merman, and his help will cost me. He already has samples of my hair and scales. I dread the walk to his house even more than usual. The place is like a fort, wrapped tightly with security.

Once I arrive, I press the button on the gate. "It's me. Let me in."

"Hello, Ryn. What a pleasant surprise," he says, buzzing me in.

Slowly, I walk up to the house. My stomach is already churning with anticipation. It hurt when he extracted a scale, and it took a long time for the imperfection to go away on my tail. Nobody else noticed, but I knew it wasn't there.

"Hello, Isaac," I say, after opening the door and going inside.

"What a pleasant surprise. Would you like some coffee, or perhaps a beer?"

"No, thank you. This isn't a social call, and I don't have much time."

"It's never a social call, but I'll drop the pretences. What can I do for you?"

"I've lost two of my good friends. One was kidnapped from the town earlier today, and the other is on a treasure hunt with a thief."

"Why not go to the police?"

"Come on, Isaac. I thought you said we're going to stop the pretences. I need these two mermaids found."

"Okay. I'll make some calls, but it's going to cost you."

I bite the inside of my mouth so the pain is still raw when I ask, "What do you want?"

"Semen."

"Excuse me?" The pain in my hand isn't enough to deal with this.

"I want you to ejaculate into a cup so I can have a look at it and maybe try some interspecies fertilisation."

"You've got to be kidding me. You can't do that."

"I never joke."

I rub my head before balling my hand into a fist. "Pick something else."

"You want me to find two rogue mermaids, and one has probably been kidnapped, so you need me to do it right now. I think the price is fair."

"You could have access to the mermaid bloodline. We're not freaks to experiment on. You're asking too much."

"If I find your girlfriend, it's probably going to cost money. How are you going to pay?"

"I never said she was my girlfriend. What do you know?" Anger races through my veins. Did he arrange for Pasha to be taken?

"Calm yourself down. I don't know anything."

"Then why do you think she's my girl?"

"You've never brought someone to shore before, and I saw you on the boat. It has a camera."

"You're a dirty pervert."

"That's no way to talk to a friend. I'm only trying to help you. The boat is mine and I need to keep an eye on it."

"What have I gotten myself into?" I mutter under my breath.

He passes me a beaker. "You go get what I want, and I'll see what the word around town is."

"I never agreed to this." I push the cup away.

"You have no choice." A wicked smile appears on his face.

I cautiously fill him in on what I know about the whereabouts of Pasha and Maris before disappearing into the small downstairs bathroom. I place the cup on the windowsill and take a piss.

Looking in the mirror, I rub my eyes. Can I really do this? If I don't do this, how am I going to get Pasha back?

Fuck.

I let my trousers fall to the floor and reach inside my boxers. It's Pasha's face and body I see as I begin to get hard. I rub quicker, letting my feelings of lust wash over me. If things were different, I'd make Pasha mine permanently, but it wouldn't be fair to either of us for me to admit how I feel because I'm a royal and she's not. Society dictates who we marry and we're not a match. I come hard, thinking about the last time we were together in my room. I pretended to be asleep when she sneaked out. Through the suffering and pain I cause, she still wants me, and it hurts because I feel the same way. I tried to convince myself we were just fooling around, but my heart tells me I'm wrong.

Once I've made the sample, I take it to Isaac. He seems to forget what's inside the beaker as he hurries it into an incubator with his bare hands. "I have some good news and some bad news," he says.

"Just tell me what you found."

"I've found the girl you were with this morning."

My gut fills with relief. "So, let's go get her."

"She was picked up by a gang of human traffickers."

"Of course she was," I say bitterly.

I'm angry she was on the truck. I'm angry with myself for letting her out of my sight, and I'm angry at the situation.

I can't lose her. Especially when she thinks I don't care.

SCORPIO
LIBRA
VIRGO
LEO

Chapter Thirteen

Aquarius is an air element

Maris

"Damn, we're in the northern hemisphere," Kasper says.

"Aquarius is seen in the southern hemisphere at this time of year," I reply.

"We travelled all the way back to Haiti for nothing." He scrunches up the page in the textbook.

"Hey, what has that library book ever done to you?" I pull it away from him.

"I'm sorry. I'm just frustrated."

"I know you are." I touch his hand, and he smiles at me.

There's something between us I've never felt before, not even with Ryn. When he looks at me like that, I get an urge to kiss him. I lick my lips, and I can see him looking. His smile wavers and his mouth copies the actions I just made. I'm mesmerised.

"The café is closing soon. You need to pack up your things," says the owner.

"Thanks," I say.

Kasper took me to the Zodiac café when the books we got from Pasha didn't hold all the answers we needed. Once we're outside, Kasper takes hold of my hand to walk me back to his house. "We need to cross the Caribbean Sea. Do you think we can do that?"

"You mean swim?" I ask.

"Yes. My boat is gone, and I don't have the money for a plane ticket. Do you think we can get there in a day or so?"

"I can call on some of my friends from the sea."

"Thank you." He kisses my cheek, and I turn my head so our lips are almost touching. "We shouldn't," he says, closing his eyes like he's in pain.

"Why not?" I ask.

"I'm not good enough for you."

"Isn't that for me to decide? Plus, it's just a kiss." I

don't understand why he thinks we shouldn't do this.

"You're sweet, beautiful, and innocent."

"Why does that sound like a bad thing?" I frown.

"It's not bad. But I'm not a guy with great moral fibre. I haven't dated anyone since high school, and I haven't gone without sex for more than two weeks."

I blush. "Did she break your heart?" Humans are different from merfolk, but still as complicated.

"You're missing the point, but yes, my high school girlfriend broke my heart."

"That's so sad." My heart hurts for him. I've never felt true heartache, and I hope I never have to.

"She did me a favour."

"What, by freezing your heart?" If he doesn't date, I'm guessing he doesn't let anyone get close.

He laughs. "By teaching me that life doesn't always work out the way you want it to."

"That doesn't mean you should give up on love."

"I love my brother. I don't need anyone else."

"I think you're wrong." Everyone needs love in their heart to be truly happy, and I don't mean just family.

"It's Owen that needs saving, not me."

"We'll see." I'm not worldly or experienced, but he's not making fun of me. I feel comfortable around Kasper, even after he turned down my advances.

He grabs hold of my waist and spins me around.

"Oh, will we?"

"Yes. Love makes the world go around. It's even written in the stars."

"Where's the evidence?"

"Zeus kidnapped Ganymede because he liked him."

He laughs. "If that's your idea of love, I think it's you who needs to protect your heart and stop daydreaming."

"He loved him so much he made him a permanent fixture in the sky."

"Zeus made him a server to the gods. He's basically a glorified waiter."

It makes me think of Ryn and Pasha. Could their situation be similar? Ryn's supposed to marry a royal or it would be frowned upon, but does he wish things were different? If he could be with Pasha, would they have told me? "Maybe Zeus couldn't make Ganymede his equal and making him the water bearer was the next best thing."

"I wouldn't want to be second-rate, and I wouldn't let anyone make me feel that way."

"Neither would I." That's why I can't marry Ryn, and the reason all my feelings turned to sadness when I realised he didn't like me in that way. He was never truly mine, and I can forgive Pasha for following her heart. I just wish she'd come to me. When I get back from this trip, I'm going to make up with her properly.

"Where did you go just then?"

"I was thinking about Pasha. I should really talk to her."

"You should if she's like family to you."

"She is." I smile sadly.

"Come on. Let's get back to Owen and make a plan to visit Brazil." I'm glad about the subject change.

"What makes you think that's where we need to be?"

"It's in the southern hemisphere, and Brazil borders onto the Atlantic Ocean."

"I've never been that far south before." It's both scary and exciting.

"Do you still want to come with me, or are you going back home?"

"I'm not turning back now."

"Good, because I need you on this."

Warmth fills my chest. I like feeling wanted, especially by him. "Maybe. Maybe not. But you don't have any choice."

"Did you miss us?" Kasper asks with a big smile. His brother is sitting in his usual chair. He looks really well, and he even has colour in his face.

"I hope you've been looking after Maris," Owen says, returning his smile.

"It's good to see you've perked up." Kasper pats him on the back. "Maris is keeping me busy, and we have another piece of the jug."

"Hello, Owen," I say.

"Don't believe everything he tells you. He will try and lead you astray." Owen leans forward and kisses me on the cheek.

"Why do you always have to be so negative? You're looking better. This is a good day." Kasper kisses his other cheek.

"I'm dying. I have good and bad days, but that remains the same," Owen says in a dry tone.

Kasper frowns.

"Hey, Owen, no need to be gloomy." I kiss his cheek again.

"You do make everything brighter, Maris. Is that a mermaid thing?" Owen asks.

"No, that's a Maris thing," Kasper says.

"You're too kind to me. Both of you are."

"He gets the kisses, though," Kasper jokes.

"You turned my kisses down."

There's a knock at the door, interrupting our conversation. Kasper pulls me into the bedroom.

"Hello," Owen says when he opens the door.

"We're looking for Kyle or Kasper Columbo."

"What's this about, Officer?" My pulse starts to race. They can't take Kasper.

"Can we come in?"

"Now's not a good time." Owen seems to be keeping his cool, and I'm grateful someone is.

"Why not?"

"Do you have a search warrant?"

"No. We just want a friendly chat."

"I'm sorry. I can't help you." The door closes.

After a few minutes, we go back into the living room.

"They had your picture. What trouble have you got yourself into now?"

"My past had to catch up with me at some point. I'll try not to draw any more attention to myself while we find the rest of the jug. We're heading to Brazil tomorrow, so we'll be out of the way."

"I'm glad you won't be here when they come back. When this is all over, we'll go back to England and turn over an honest leaf."

"Yes. That's what I want too." They hug.

When this is all over, will I have found what I was looking for? Will I have learnt anything, or will I go back to my palace under the sea and continue to feel like something is missing?

SCORPIO
LIBRA
VIRGO

Chapter Fourteen

If an Aquarius ever cared about someone, it's likely they still do

Ryn

"Put on the suit and try not to speak when we get there."

I do what Isaac wants. "Why do we need to wear these clothes?" I ask.

"We're going to pretend we're after some girls for a new club."

"That's sick, even by your standards." The thought makes my stomach queasy.

"Do you have a better idea of how to get her back?"

"No."

"Then let's go."

A short car journey later, we're at a desolate warehouse. I brush my hair back and follow Isaac inside. A group of men in suits waits inside. I look around, hoping to see Pasha or any of the girls they have here, but they must be somewhere else.

"Mr Anderson. Nice to see you again," one of the men says to Isaac. This isn't the first time he's been here, and I'm not surprised.

"Where are you storing the merchandise?"

"We have some lovely ladies here," he says.

"But not all?" I ask. Isaac gives me a warning look.

"We've just made a big shipment that's on its way to Mexico."

Panic rises within me. "I need to see the women now."

"Keep your cool, Ryn. Mr Black will have what you're looking for." He turns to give the guy his full attention. "His wife recently passed away, and he's looking to replace her with someone who looks similar."

"She must have been really special."

I clench my fist but push my anger back down. I need to get Pasha and get out of here before I do something stupid. "Let's see what you have," I say.

"Right this way, men." He leads us into a cooler area behind hanging meat hooks. There are trays of ice for fish on the sides, and I shudder. One of Mr Black's men opens the cooler, and we follow him inside. The girls are all huddled together, but as I glance at each face, I realise Pasha isn't here.

"When did the other girls leave?" I ask, trying to hold my temper.

"About twenty minutes ago."

"Bring them back now."

"I can get a custom order if you give me a picture."

"How about you give us the registration of the truck, and if we pick something, we'll pay double," Isaac says.

"I want someone today," I say, trying to play along, but honestly, I'm struggling to hold it together. Pasha is on her way to Mexico, probably in a cooler like this. What if she transforms into a mermaid when she gets too cold?

"I'll give you the GPS details, but I'll want three times the price."

"It's going to cost you," Isaac says to me.

I close my eyes and slowly breathe out of my nose. "Fine. Let's just get this done."

He shakes hands with Mr Black, and we leave the warehouse. "Are you sure the girl's worth it?" Isaac asks.

I need her back, and I'm struggling to hide my desperation. "Can't we steal her?"

"He will know it's us. I'll pay the money, and you'll

pay me." He's void of emotion as usual, and I feel like I'm losing control.

"I've already given you a deposit." What more is it going to cost me?

"The stakes just went up, and you need to compensate me."

"And what's the price?" I can't show how much saving her means to me or he'll use it to his advantage.

"A sperm donation a month for six months."

"That's too high." If only he knew I'd pay anything. I don't want to give him any bodily fluids, especially if he can use it to make children.

"And a scale."

"Go to hell."

"Don't worry, I will. Now, agree to my terms or stop wasting my time."

"Fuck." I kick the dirt. If I didn't have feelings for her this would be so much simpler and I'd be able to leave her there until I'd bartered the price.

When did my life get so complicated? All I had to do was marry Maris and the kingdom would have been mine. Why did I have to fuck it up? Now, not only will I be jerking off for Isaac, I'll probably lose both girls. I slap my cheek, hoping I can snap out of this pity party. That's not me. I'm selfish and I go after what I want.

"Let's go get my girl," I say because, deep down, that's what I want and need to do.

"As you wish."

We write the coordinates into the mapping system and put a track on the truck's GPS. Mr Black lied. The truck has an hour on us, and we need to hurry if we're going to catch them up. We hit the motorway at breakneck speed and zoom down the road. Isaac is a man on a mission when he wants something, and I try not to think about what that means for me.

When the truck comes into view, Isaac tries to get the driver to pull over, but he almost runs us off the road. We follow him for a couple of miles and his driving gets erratic. "Can't we contact him?"

"If it was that simple, Mr Black would've given us the number."

"So what do we do?"

"Maybe we should drop back and hope he calms down."

"What if we lose them?"

"We have the GPS information. We need to wait for him to stop."

"Okay. Do it."

It feels like we've been following them for days. I'm frustrated, and the pressure is getting to me. I fidget in my seat.

"We need to stop for petrol and the bathroom," Isaac says.

"No."

"Sorry, Ryn. You're not the one in control. It'll take ten minutes and then we'll be back on the road."

"Just hurry up."

He pulls into the petrol station and gets out, turning the car off. I watch him fill up and disappear inside.

Drumming my fingers against the dashboard, I wait for him to come back. Why is nothing going my way? The tips of my fingers begin to ache from the force of my tapping. When Isaac returns, I'm ready to explode. "Come on!" I bark.

He climbs into the car and turns the key. The vehicle roars to life and the GPS turns back on. "We have a problem," he says as he pulls out of the station.

"What could possibly be wrong now?" My tone is borderline aggressive, but I've had enough of today.

"The truck seems to have gone off the radar." He taps the navigation system, drawing my eyes to the searching icon.

"Can someone please give me a break?" I say, more to myself than Isaac.

"Relax. It probably means they've stopped. We've just got to work out where."

"If we hadn't dropped back it might be a little easier."

"They can't have gone far. We'll go to the last known coordinates and take it from there." He puts his foot down on the gas.

We get to the location, and I get my first glimpse of luck. The vehicle is parked up in a nearby layby.

Isaac parks in front of the truck. "Let's talk to the driver first so you don't startle him. Try and calm your temper."

"Fine," I bite out.

The guy in question is taking a piss when we find him in between the trees. Isaac holds his hands up, and I copy him. "Mr Black sent us," he says.

"Can't a guy catch a two-minute break to relieve himself?"

"Sorry," I say. "But I think you have something we need."

After we explain why we're here, he lets us into the back of the truck. It's a cooler like the one at the warehouse, and everyone looks cold. I've never really cared about anyone but myself, but I wish I could help these women. Unfortunately, Pasha isn't here either, and I have to walk away.

"Did any of the girls from the warehouse go anywhere else?" Isaac asks.

"I'm just a delivery driver."

"But you know something?" I ask.

Isaac opens his wallet and hands over some money.

"It's not worth my life to tell you," the driver says, shaking his head.

"We won't tell anyone where we got our information from," Isaac says, offering him more money.

"Fine. One girl was taken to a special customer."

"Do you have an address?" I ask.

He rubs his face. "Blake House."

"Where's that?" I ask.

"Thank you," Isaac says, handing over even more cash. He walks back to the car, and I follow.

"What's Blake House?" I ask.

"A cult," Isaac says.

Holy crap. *What have you got yourself into, Pasha?*

LEO
VIRGO
LIBRA
SCORPIO

Chapter Fifteen

Aquarians Believe in True Love

Maris

Relaxing under the stars in Brazil is magical. After sending a call out to some friends, we got a ride to Rio de Janeiro. Once the dolphins left us on the beach, it was late, so we made a campfire and I caught us some fish.

"I thought the marine life were your friends," Kasper says.

"Yes, they are, and we only eat certain kinds of food, not our friends," I reply.

"I guess that's like on land. We have pets here, and they're family, not food."

"Do you think you'll have a pet when you move back to England?"

"Not unless my brother wants one. I'd like a steady job instead of having to hide all the time."

We eat the fish and disregard the bones.

"Why did the authorities what to speak with you?"

"I already told you. I've done things I'm not proud of. My past is finally catching up with me, and I've probably outstayed my welcome in Haiti."

"I'm guessing there's no chance of you visiting me, then?"

"Aww. Do you think you'll miss me, princess?"

"Yes. You've been the most real person with me."

"I'm sure you'll find your place when you return home. Do you think your father will be worried about you?"

"He's probably going out of his mind." We lie down, staring at the stars.

"Then why did you continue this journey with me?"

"Because I'm angry he still wants me to marry Ryn, and he needs to know I can make my own decisions. While I'm on land, I'm not under his ruling, and I need this space as much as he does."

"And what if you're wrong and he doesn't let you leave his side again?"

"I'm no longer going to let anyone tell me what to do. I'm old enough to shape my own future."

"You're cute when you're bossy."

"I prefer the term *assertive.*"

"Okay, Miss Independent, what's your plan for getting the next piece of the jug?"

"The Aquarius constellation is right there." I point to the stars in the sky, then to the screwed-up drawing that got damaged on the way here. "See."

"We have the sea, sand, and stars. Maybe the piece will just appear."

"That would be lucky. I have noticed something else happens when we get a piece."

"Oh, yeah. What's that?"

"It might be nothing, but have you noticed we always seem close when we uncover a secret?"

"We're always together?"

"More than together. Both times we've almost been kissing."

"Is this your way of saying you want to make out?"

"Nope. You already turned me down once. I only want to kiss men who want to kiss me back."

"I never said I didn't want to kiss you. You're worth more than me or Ryn."

"That's just something people say when they're not really interested."

"That's not true at all. It's not that I don't want you. Actually, I want too much. I couldn't stop at one kiss. I want to touch. I want to wrap my body around yours and take things that don't belong to me."

"I'm sick of everyone treating me like a child."

"I thought I was the only one that was real with you."

"Yes. You've explained you don't think you're a nice guy, but you never gave me the chance to make my own mind up about you."

"Fine. Tell me what you think of me."

"I think you're brave and scared. You're courageous because you're doing everything you can to save your brother, even if it breaks ethics. You wish it didn't, but you're also scared you're losing yourself."

"That's deep."

"I'm not just a pretty face."

"You're definitely not. If finding the jug means we have to romance under Aquarius, I'll try to control myself."

"Nope. You've missed your chance to prove my theory now."

"Oh, is that right?" He sits up, and I look at him

curiously to see what he's going to do. He stands towering over me, and I can't help but smile.

"Am I in trouble?" Other than getting my attention, I'm not sure why he's standing in front of the stars.

"Do you want to be?"

I bite my lip, suddenly feeling nervous, but he doesn't comfort me like he usually would.

"Stop messing around."

He shakes his head, shaking off whatever he was about to do. "Come on. Let's go for a walk under the stars before we snuggle in for the night."

We brought a simple cloth tent with us, which we've put up behind some nearby rocks. "That sounds like a plan."

He offers me a hand and pulls me to my feet. We start to walk.

"What's more romantic, a walk or a swim?" he asks.

"I like the sand between my toes. What about you?"

"The beach is pretty, and you can watch the sunset behind the waves."

"See? I knew you were a softy underneath the tough guy act."

"Just don't tell anyone."

I laugh. "If you could visit anywhere in the world, where would it be?"

"You already know the answer to that."

"The lost city of Atlantis?"

"Yes."

"Before we go our separate ways, I'll have to show you my city."

"I'd like that. How do you think we're going to solve the next clue to finding the jug?"

"Tomorrow we should walk the coast, looking for a picture of Aquarius."

"That sounds like a good idea."

"Better than kissing?"

He laughs. "We'll find the carving or painting of the stars, then we'll try kissing."

It's my turn to laugh. "If all else fails."

We continue our walk and arrive back at the tent in time for bed. We sit and watch the stars for a while, and our conversation stays light.

"It's getting late. I'm going to fall asleep," I say.

"I'll let you change, then I'll join you."

I nod and enter the tent. My jeans and t-shirt are traded for a long t-shirt before I snuggle into the thin sheet. "I'm ready," I say.

Kasper gets in next to me and removes his jeans. "Goodnight, Maris."

"Sweet dreams," Kasper.

He kisses my cheek and cuddles up to me. I fall asleep easily, thinking of the stars and Kasper.

SCORPIO
LIBRA
VIRGO
LEO

Chapter Sixteen

Amethyst is the birthstone of Aquarius

Pasha

The rope around my wrists is so tight I can't entertain the idea of wriggling free. The throb that's going to come if they ever take it off is playing on my mind. *Oh, Gods. Don't let me die.* I've been travelling most of the day, but it doesn't feel like I've got very far. The men that took me have had me under a microscope and taken samples of my blood. Now I'm back in the boot of a car—as one of the guys called it—with a bag over my head. The road starts to get rocky and my body bounces around like a ragdoll. The car jolts to a stop, and I go flying to the back of the boot. It's no longer just my wrists that hurt.

The doors to the vehicle open and shut. There are male voices all around the car, and my heart starts to beat faster. The truck opens, and my flight response kicks in. I lash out in all directions, trying to get away. They pull me out of the car, and I fall with a thud to the floor. It's no use. I can't get away. Someone holds me down while another person pulls the bag off my head. The light from the sun is so bright my vision is temporarily lost.

"Pasha," a guy says.

"Let me go!" I shout.

"Calm down."

"I'll calm down when you let me go." I try to struggle again.

"Guys, give her some space."

The other men move back and I sit up. "Someone untie me," I say, holding my wrists out. I have no idea if they will, but I need these damn ropes off. The oldest of the men gestures for someone to do it, and I rub my arms as I'm finally free. Well, not free, but not restrained anymore. They're all staring at me like I have something on my face. "How did you know my name?" I ask.

"That's not important right now. We need to clean you up. Those men should've looked after you better. Come. We'll go inside." He starts to walk and the others follow. I look at the massive white house in front of me, then back at the driveway.

Would they stop me from leaving?

They don't look back as they walk away. I doubt I can outrun them all, and it's probably a false delusion I can get away. This might be stupid, but I follow them inside. The walls are full of pictures of marine life, and there are fish tanks everywhere.

"Come," a woman says. She doesn't look like a prisoner, and I start to relax a bit.

"I'm Pasha," I say, hoping she can ease my mind.

"I know who you are," she says, giving nothing away. She leads me to a bedroom with a view of the sea and leaves me. I look out the window, missing my home. There's a bathroom attached to the room, and I use it to freshen up. When I come out, there are clothes laid out on the bed. I'm hesitant to change, but everything I have on doesn't belong to me, and these clothes are much softer. Once dressed in the white top and grey bottoms, I sit on the bed, wondering if anyone will come to collect me. Sitting turns to lying, and I'm so tired I drift off to sleep.

A knock at the door awakens me. I wipe my face and rush to get up. The bed's so comfy I almost forgot where I was.

"Pasha," the woman from before says, letting herself into the room. "Dinner's ready. Are you coming down to join us, or do you want me to bring something up?"

My stomach growls, and I'm grateful I'm going to be fed. I'm curious what these people want with me. "I'll come down," I say.

She nods and I follow her. "Find a spare seat and someone will bring you a plate," she says.

I take the seat closest to the door. The dining hall is full of people of all ages, who are talking and eating. This doesn't have a prison feel at all. I help myself to a bread roll and keep my head down until the older guy from before enters the room. Heads turn to look at him, including mine.

"Evening all," he says. "Pasha," he adds as he catches my eye. He takes his seat at the head of the table and the food is served.

I eat until I feel like I'm going to burst. The food is so rich and tasty. My name keeps being whispered around the table, but I try to ignore it.

After a while, people start to leave until only the older guy and I are left. "How was the food?" he asks.

"Nice, thank you," I say.

"Good. I'm glad. Shall we take a walk?"

"Are you going to kill me?" Surely it's better to know what he wants than to wonder how much trouble I'm in.

He laughs, but it's strangled. "No. I love you."

My eyes widen. What's going on here? "How can you love someone you just met?" The air suddenly feels close and I start to hyperventilate. I fan my face, trying to take in deeper breaths.

"We've met before," he says, shaking his head. Should I remember him? I've never been on land before. How could he know who I am? I try to ask another question, but he silences me with his finger, which is probably best as I'm not in any shape to talk yet. "Let's walk and then we'll talk."

I follow him for the second time today without much resistance. "Tell me your name," I say once I can.

"My name is Neptune," he says.

It's a popular merman name, but I feel like I should know this man. That was my father's name, and it's not a human name as far as I'm aware. "Neptune," I repeat.

"Did your mum ever talk about your dad?" he asks, and my stomach flips over.

"He left us," I say.

"Did she tell you why?"

All the answers my mother ever gave me were more

like digs at my father. She never gave me a real reason. I twist my hair into a knot around my fingers, hoping it will offer comfort. Is my dad a land dweller? "No."

"Do you ever feel there could be more than what's under the sea?" He coughs. "Of course you do or you wouldn't be here."

"You know what I am?" I ask.

"Can't you tell?" He looks around like I'm missing something big.

I look at the guys by the pool and the women with their legs dipped in the water. Children are running around and having fun, and I smile. The woman who showed me upstairs lifts her dress above her head and jumps into the pool. A flash of blue shimmers across the waves. "Mermaid," I say.

"We're all part of the rebellion, and we're all mer."

I look back at Neptune. "Dad?"

"Yes." He hugs me tight, and I can hear the sob in the back of his throat. "I thought I'd never see you again."

"That makes two of us. Does Mum know where you are?"

"It was her choice to stay behind."

Why would Mum choose to work in the factory instead of exploring this possibility? It might not be under the sea, but these people look free.

SCORPIO
LIBRA
VIRGO
LEO

Chapter Seventeen

The ruling planet of Aquarius is Uranus

Kasper

For two days, we've been walking the beaches of Brazil. Don't get me wrong, I love spending time with Maris, but when are we going to find a clue? I need to get back to my brother, not feel like I'm on a romantic getaway.

"I think I've found something," Maris says.

"Where?" I look around. We've been standing next to each other the whole time, so what could I have missed?

"We have a god who stood before us with his hands out wide."

"Yes, but he isn't a Greek god."

"Who says he has to be? Aquarius features in the Bible."

"Are you saying I need to believe in Jesus?"

"We're not talking about your spiritual path. Although, that's kind of what the text said. If you believe in him, water will flow out of his body. We're standing on Copacabana Beach looking at the guy in question. That must be the sign." She points to the statue of Jesus Christ at Corcovado. It looks much smaller than when I visited it up close a couple of years ago, but she's right. We are in the presence of a god.

"I was hoping for some tiny stars." The blue obsidian and star-like holes in the cave were so much simpler than trying to align the stars with the ocean and landscape.

"You have them in the sky." She's confident she's right, and it's sexy to see her like this.

"The other two clues were easier."

She shrugs. "I told you we almost kissed both times."

"There you go, trying to seduce me again." I laugh. At least it's not just me thinking in a non-platonic way.

"You're impossible." She shakes her hands like she's pretending to be mad, but her smile gives her away.

"What you're saying is the jug needs romance under Aquarius." I pick a shell up from the sand and pass it to her.

"Do you have any better ideas, Mr Pessimistic?"

"I'm not that bad." Here I was thinking we were flirty when she shuts me down for being gloomy. I guess a shell isn't really romantic, even for a mermaid.

"Okay." I playfully nudge her leg with my foot.

"What?" She smiles in that beautiful way she does when she's being mischievous.

"Tonight, you and I are going to kiss until your lips are swollen," I say boldly. My dick twitches and my pulse quickens.

"I thought you couldn't control yourself."

If I let my dick do the talking, then she's right, but I'd never hurt her. I couldn't because she's too important to me. "Maybe I'm not as bad as I made out. I was trying to protect your innocence."

She lets out a weird laugh. "You worry about yourself and leave me to seduce men who aren't interested."

Anger flashes through me. Her ex really did a number on her if that's what she thinks. "Don't do that. Ryn was an asshole, but there are good guys out there."

"But not you."

She's making me want to be better, and once this is over, I won't be playing games with women again, but I have to be truthful. “Nope, not me. I’ll be honest with you. When we find the jug and save my brother, I’m going to move back to England. If you’re okay with that, I’ll give you as much or as little of myself as you want.”

“Why?” She frowns. I’m unsure what she’s asking at first, but I want her to know she’s not just some girl to me.

“Because you’re beautiful. Not in the flaky type of way that I usually date. You’re real, Maris, and you deserve a guy who is just as great.”

“You’ve flown halfway across the world to save your brother and you’ve given up everything holding onto the hope you can find a cure. I think that makes you a special person.”

I like the way she sees me, and it brings a smile to my face. Taking her hand in mine, I pull her towards me for a chaste kiss. It’s soft and feels natural to be doing this. We spend the rest of the day finding the perfect location on Copacabana Beach. Once the statues are in sight and the stars begin to come out, we settle on a blanket, waiting for the right moment.

“I really like Brazil,” Maris says.

“What makes it so special for you?”

“It’s beautiful and romantic.”

“I guess it is.” I touch her hand. “I’ve enjoyed sleeping under the stars with you.”

"Me too." She leans in and kisses me softly.

It feels like it's just me and her. The people and elements around us fade away. I look deep into her ocean blue eyes and keep my promise. We kiss for what feels like most of the night.

"Are you getting cold?" I ask.

"I've never really felt a chill before. Maybe tonight I need to take a swim in my true form."

"I could come with you or watch from the beach?" I rub her arms, trying to warm her and hide my worry.

"You wait here and I'll be back." She goes to the edge of the beach and strips down.

I should turn away, but I don't. She dives into the water and disappears under the waves. I already miss having her next to me. I leave the blanket and walk along the tiny waves as they rise up onto the sand. The moon is out in its full glory and Aquarius is beaming down on me.

Removing my clothes, I wade into the water to try and catch a glimpse of Maris. I'm in up to my shoulder by the time I see her beautiful tail swim by. She grabs hold of my ankles and slithers up my body until she's facing me eye to eye. "Do you feel better?" I ask.

"Yes." She wraps her arms around my neck and pulls me into a deep kiss. My arms wrap around her waist, and

I stroke the scales of her tail. If she notices my erection, she doesn't say anything.

We kiss in the water and continue our lip-locking session on land. Romancing under Aquarius has become the most unforgettable night of my life.

When I wake in the early hours, Maris has warmed to her usual temperature and the answer to my prayers is right in between us. The next piece of the jug has appeared just like magic.

SCORPIO
LIBRA
VIRGO
LEO

Chapter Eighteen

Aquarius is the eleventh zodiac sign

Ryn

My heart is in my throat by the time we reach Blake House. I'm never letting Pasha out of my sight again once I find her. They say absence makes the heart grow fonder, but worrying about someone you love is far worse. I've tried to play down my feelings and now I'm full of regret. She doesn't know I even like her. I'm going out of my mind and I need to fix this.

Isaac pulls up at the black iron gate of Blake House

and cuts the engine. "What now?" I ask, taking in the huge white house.

"We need to get out of the car and stand with our hands up so they know we're not a threat."

"Okay." We do as he suggested, but there's no sign that anyone is paying attention. "Shouldn't we ring the doorbell or something?"

"Blake House will be the judge of who can enter."

I frown, letting my arms drop a fraction. "Why are you talking like that?"

"I've tried to get an audience with the owner for years with no luck."

"Then how are we going to get inside?" I grit my teeth. If Pasha's here, I need to see her.

"Like I said. We have to wait."

I throw my hands out to the sides. "How long?"

"As long as it takes."

I'm practically pulling my hair out and ready to scale the wall by the time the gate opens. "Finally," I say. I look at Isaac, who shakes his head, warning me not to move.

A man leaves the house and walks towards us. He takes out a magnifying glass and looks into the irises of our eyes. I thought Isaac was freaky, but this guy takes it to a new level. What could he be looking for?

"You can come in, but your friend must wait here," he says to me.

"Look, man, I'm just looking for my girlfriend. Has a tall brunette by the name of Pasha stopped by recently?"

"You idiot. You've just shown your whole hand," Isaac says.

"If she's in there, how am I going to get her out on my own with you waiting outside?" I ask.

"Good question. Why don't you go find out?"

I rub my head. My frustration turns into fear. Isaac doesn't exactly sell the human world as a friendly place. The first time he caught me on land, he started to tempt me with things I could only dream of, but there was always a price.

The guy hasn't answered my question and doesn't look like he's going to. Isaac can't help me anymore, and I have no choice but to enter Blake House with the stranger.

The iron gate closes behind us and Issacs's tyres screech. The asshole has left me here.

We go inside, and the guy leads me into the back garden. He's older than me and has white strands mixed in with his brown hair. He looks athletic but he wouldn't be a match for me. There are people everywhere once we're outside, and I'd have to run fast if they picked a fight with me. I look around, but I can't see Pasha. Blake House doesn't look like the cults I've seen on TV. This place is more like a holiday resort. He leads me into a small hut and gestures for me to take a seat. I tap my knee, hoping I'm given answers soon.

"I'm Neptune," a guy says when someone finally comes back. He's also an older guy with white in his hair.

"Where's Pasha?" I ask.

"Don't worry. She's safe."

"Please let me see her."

"I will in a moment. First, I have some questions. You told the guard she's your girlfriend."

"Yes. We got separated and I just want her back." My voice breaks in desperation.

"Tell me about her." He sits on the desk in front of me.

"Look, asshole, I've been running all over Haiti looking for her. I don't have time for games."

"Humour me."

"She's kind, creative, and ambitious. She's the only person I know who doesn't conform to her fate and her beauty is second to none." I'm standing by the time I've finished talking. I've never admitted that to anyone before.

"You really love her?"

"Yes, I do."

"Does she know how you feel?"

I hang my head in shame. "No. I've been a shitty

boyfriend, but if you let me take her home, I'll make it up to her."

"I can't promise she'll leave with you, but I'll show you where she is."

I nod, trying to process his words. Why wouldn't she want to leave with me? Once I've seen her, I can sort out whatever difficulties we have.

He leads me to the pool where I zone in on Pasha in a bathing suit, drinking a cocktail and laughing with some woman.

"What the fuck are you doing?" I bark once I'm close enough.

She spills her drink as she sits up. "Ryn. What are you doing here?"

"What am I doing here? I've been worried sick. I've visited brothels and drug cartels trying to hunt you down, and you're sitting here like you're on holiday." I thrust my fist down by my side.

"He's handsome, Pasha," one of the women says with a giggle.

"He knows it, though." She sighs heavily.

"Are you drunk?" I knit my eyebrows together.

She squeezes her index finger and thumb together. "Maybe a little."

I rub my eye. "It's time to go home."

"We were banished, remember?"

"All we need to do is find Maris and then we can go."

"Oh, yes. Home's the only place you'd want to be." She takes a bow.

"I can't talk to you when you're like this."

"Then stop talking and start drinking. It's okay. We're amongst friends here." She spills her drink again as she gestures around us.

"How are these strangers our friends?"

She covers the side of her mouth and attempts to whisper. "This is a mer sanctuary."

I shake my head. That can't be true, but as I start to look around, the truth is there to see. The swimmers in the pool are mermaids. "Okay, so you're right, but it doesn't change anything."

"Is he always this grumpy?" the mermaid asks.

Pasha laughs. "Yes. He is."

"Hey, that's not fair."

"Then stop being so serious and relax. We're not going anywhere tonight, so chill out. Grab a beer."

She's probably right. Even if I dragged her out of here, we wouldn't get very far. Isaac left us, and I don't know where to start looking for Maris. If we stick around, maybe someone here can help us. I take a seat on a nearby lounger but don't accept any drink offers.

The guy who showed me to Pasha returns an hour

later. "Have you and your boyfriend managed to catch up?"

"He's not my boyfriend," she replies.

"Sorry. He said he was."

She looks at me and rolls her eyes. Is she mad at me? It doesn't matter because she probably won't remember tomorrow, and I can't have the conversation with her now. "I'm a close friend," I say. My usual vague answer isn't really cutting it anymore.

"Will your friend be staying for dinner?" the guy asks Pasha.

"Yes," Pasha says.

I want to ask her what's going on. Are we free to leave? Does she want to stay with these merpeople, or is she just drunk?

We walk together to the food hall and sit opposite each other. The guy I think is the leader, Neptune, welcomes everyone to eat, and I dig in.

"Where will I be sleeping tonight?" I ask.

"I think there's a rug in my room," Pasha says.

"Ouch. Are you mad at me for letting those guys take you?"

"No. I'm mad at you showing up here and thinking you can play the boyfriend card."

"I'm sorry."

"If we were home, you'd never introduce yourself like that."

"You're right. I'm sorry." We can have a more in-depth conversation later, but I owe her at least an apology for the way I've behaved.

SCORPIO
LIBRA
VIRGO
LEO

Chapter Nineteen

The Water Bearer Symbolises Truth and Pure Intentions

Maris

"A handle and two pieces of the jug is great," I say.

"Yes, but we didn't get a clue where the other two pieces are," Kasper says.

"What should we do now we're back in Haiti?"

"I think we need to check on my brother first. Then look for a hidden clue or something because we're at a dead end."

"Maybe if we fit the pieces together... we might have missed something." Kasper's been looking for a way to find the next piece since he realised it wasn't going to be so easy.

"Yes, that's a good idea."

We make our way to his house and it's quiet when we go inside. "Shit. Owen." He rushes to where his brother is lying on the floor. "Call 118 and ask for an ambulance. The address is written on the letter on the table," he says.

I pick up a mobile phone from the table and make the call for help.

Kasper lowers his chin to his chest. "Will you go with him?" he asks, putting his hands together in a plea.

"What about you?"

"I'm wanted, remember?"

"Okay. Yes, I'll go." We kiss goodbye, and I hate the pain on his face. I wish I could take it away for both of them.

When asked about medical insurance, I had to improvise by handing over my pearl earrings and necklace to a local pawn shop. I had to leave Owen while I figured out what to do, but I'm proud I could solve the problem without worrying Kasper. Once Owen's stable, I sit with him, waiting for him to wake up. He looks peaceful but frail.

I stroke his hand, needing the comfort. Compared with my own life, Kasper and Owen have it so much harder. My father's probably worried about me, and when I get home, I'm going to tell him how much I love him. He's always been my rock, even if we haven't agreed on things. I want him to be proud of me, and I'm going to talk to him about making my own decisions. Being here with Owen is making me miss him.

The doctor enters the room and pulls back the curtains to let some light into the room. He opens the window and checks Owen's chart. "We've done the best we can for him, Ms Columbo," he says, addressing me as his sister. Only family members are allowed to be with the patients, so I had to improvise.

"Thank you, Doctor. When will he wake?" I ask.

"Hopefully soon, but there's not much else we can do for him." He smiles, but it's full of empathy.

I knew Owen was dying, but having someone spell it out makes it more real. He's so young, and he seems so awesome. I don't want him to go. Finding the jug is becoming important to me too. I want to save him. I'd like more time with them both, even if they're moving back to England.

I'm left alone with my thoughts again and a tear slips down my face. I'm torn between wanting to go find the Aquarius clues and spend my time with Owen. I'm beginning to understand Kasper's position. It must be tearing him apart.

It's a couple more hours before Owen wakes, and I immediately alert the team to check on him. Once the doctor and nurse leave us alone, I say, "You gave us a scare."

"Where is my brother?"

"He thought it best he stayed away."

"Did you manage to find what you were looking for in Brazil?"

"Yes. We just need two more pieces."

"That's not what I meant." He turns his head to look at me. "He's going to need someone when I'm gone." His lip quivers and I reach out to take his hand. Our fingers interlock and I hold on tight.

"Don't talk like that," I say. The first tear falls, and it's like a floodgate opens as they start to stream down my face.

I'm not ready to let go. I feel like I've known Owen and Kasper a lot longer than I actually have. They mean more to me than merfolk I've known my whole life.

"It's my time, Maris." He slumps his shoulders down.

"No, it's not. We're going to find the jug." I shake my head, refusing to give up.

He rubs my hand. "But if you don't, make sure Kasper knows it's okay."

"Okay." I nod. I don't want to think I might have to do what he's asking, but if I do, I'll be there for Kasper.

"Hand me my shirt."

I blink a few times. Why does he want to get changed? "You can't leave."

"I have no desire to spend my final days in here." He straightens up his posture.

"We can't look for the jug and keep our eye on you." I feel bad as soon as the words are out.

"I'm an adult. I don't need a babysitter."

"Yes, but you're sick." I'm making it worse, but I can't find the right words.

He sucks in a breath then blows it out. He looks deep into my eyes. "What do you want from life?"

His question catches me off guard. "Excuse me?"

"What's the one thing that will make you happy?"

"I... I... I don't have an answer."

"And I don't have time to figure out what I would've liked. But right now, I'd like to see the ocean and enjoy the sun on my face. You can't deny a dying man."

My eyes widen. "I'm sorry."

"Don't take everything so seriously. Now pass me my shirt."

"But..."

"You heard what the doc said. They can only make

me comfortable, but they can't do any more to help my condition."

"He can check on you here."

"I already told you, I don't need a babysitter."

"If something happens, you need to be here."

"I'm dying. Don't let me waste the rest of my time cooped up."

I'm out of arguments, and to be honest, I can see his point. "Fine." Swiping his shirt off the arm of the chair, I hand it to him. He puts on his trousers and shoes. I look away when he removes the hospital gown, but he tuts at me.

"We're practically family, Maris."

I smile. "I wouldn't want to make things uncomfortable by staring at you."

"Why? As soon as someone finds out I'm sick, they look at me differently anyway."

"You're still a guy."

"Funny nobody else seems to see me that way anymore. Are you sure about that?"

"Okay, I get it. Let's go to the beach, and I'll call your brother to meet us there."

"I knew you were my kind of girl."

"Remember that when your brother's telling me off for breaking you out."

Sunbathing with these two guys should be so much fun. Owen made me promise we'd have one normal day, and I intend to grant the wish.

"I feel lucky to be out with you beautiful men. I'm the envy of every woman here," I say hoping, Owen knows I see him as more than a sick person.

Owen laughs. "I think the women are jealous of you and wish the men would pay them some attention."

"Are you hitting on Maris?" Kasper asks, making Owen and me laugh.

"He used to be jealous of all the girls I used to get," Owen says, nudging me.

"Once the jug's fixed, you'll be back to having all the girls lining up."

"He lost his touch long before we came here," Kasper says, smirking.

"Are you jealous, brother?" Owen asks, the humour staying in his voice.

"No," Kasper says too fast, earning him another laugh.

"Okay, so picture this. Two carefree guys lying on a beach. Which one are you drawn to, Maris?"

He's only playing with Kasper, but I don't know

what his goal is. “I would be looking at the ocean, where I’d be swimming.”

“Boo. I thought you were fun,” Owen jokes.

“Fine, I’ll play. I’d totally drool over you both.”

Owen laughs hard, and Kasper frowns. “We’re just fucking with you,” Owen tells his brother. “I miss the days when everything wasn’t so serious.”

“Okay. Let’s stop hitting on Maris and get a beer,” Kasper says.

“Yes, let’s do it,” Owen agrees.

We spend the rest of the day trying to be merrier and forgetting our troubles.

SCORPIO
LIBRA
VIRGO

Chapter Twenty

AQUARIANS LIVE HAPPILY IN THEIR OWN HEAD

Pasha

My head hurts like I've been hit by a hammer shark. I open one eye and try to sit up, but the room starts to spin. The awful taste in my mouth makes me retch. I'm never drinking human poison again. "When will the pain stop?" I ask, holding my head.

I don't expect a response, so Ryn makes me jump when he says, "I told you that you'd regret drinking that last glass of wine."

I lift the covers to discover I'm naked. "Please tell me nothing happened between us last night."

"I've seen you nude before."

"Yes, but I've decided we can't do that again."

"Oh, have you?" He leans closer, pressing his naked body to mine.

"Come any closer and I'll be sick."

"I'll get you some water." He moves to the edge of the bed and pours me a glass from a jug on the side. I sit up to drink it while watching him. Ryn isn't usually this attentive.

"Thanks," I say, taking a few sips. "Did I do anything embarrassing last night?"

"Other than practically disowning me and declaring you're done with men? No."

"Those are strong words, but I'm serious about ending our non-relationship. I won't be played any longer."

"When I thought you'd been taken by a group of human traffickers, I was going out of my mind with worry, and it's made me realise how strong my feelings are for you."

"Save your speech. I'm not changing my mind because however you feel doesn't affect the outcome. You're part of the royal court, and I'm an outcast."

"It's not that simple."

"When we get home, will you go back to your life like nothing's happened?"

"We have to return to normal."

"You might, but I have options."

He thrusts his arms down by his sides, letting out a frustrated groan. "You can't be seriously thinking about staying here."

"He's my dad, and I don't want to work at the factory. Why shouldn't I consider this place as an option?"

"Because these people are strangers. Your family and friends are back in Atlantis."

"I'm not a princess or even a royal. My future in Atlantis is bleak. My dad is the leader of the rebellion. Here, I might find an important place."

"What's to rebel against?"

"You wouldn't understand because you're privileged."

"So tell me."

"Every member of your family has the opportunity to live their dreams and get a great job. You and your sister will marry well and have a beautiful cave. All I can hope for is my own place, and if I'm lucky, a hard-working husband that doesn't leave me."

"It's not easy for me. I don't have a choice over who I marry or the job I'm given."

"It's better than the factory."

"It's all part of the cognitive circle of life. Everyone has to do their bit."

"In Atlantis it is. Here, I could have more."

"What about Maris?" He holds his hands up like I've forgotten the reason we're here in the first place.

"She not the naïve girl you think she is. She can handle herself."

"You're going to abandon her?" He raises his voice, and my head begins to pound.

"Quieten down."

"You're going to leave her out there and leave me?" He frowns, then rubs his head.

"Technically, you'll be leaving me."

"That's not fair."

"You make out you have these deep feelings for me, but really, what you're doing is choosing Maris."

"You're being crazy right now." He closes his eyes for a few seconds.

"If we go back to Atlantis, we have no future together."

"What do you know about the people we're staying with? What if everything isn't quite as it seems?"

"If I don't give them a chance, I won't know."

There's a knock at the door and someone says, "Breakfast is ready."

"Are you coming down or are you feeling too tender? I could bring you something back," Ryn says, climbing out of the bed and getting dressed. I can't help but check out his ass.

"I'll come down," I say.

Slowly, I climb from the bed and get dressed. I catch Ryn staring, but I don't comment. A second ago, I did the same thing.

We go downstairs and join the others at the table. I've learnt some of their names, but there are over fifty mer of all ages living here. It'll take me a while to remember everyone.

"I've heard a rumour," my dad says, taking a drink of his coffee.

"Oh yeah? What's that?" I help myself to a bagel and some soft cheese.

"The king's daughter might be on land helping a human."

I glance at Ryn, who's plating some food. "Oh. What did you hear?" he asks.

"Apparently, she was on the beach with two human guys yesterday."

"Two?" I ask.

"Yes. Do you know anything about the princess's whereabouts?"

Ryn touches my arm in warning. He stares deep into my eyes, and I answer a little more cautiously. "Maris isn't a threat to this place. She's a good girl."

"If the princess is on land unprotected, we could use it to our advantage. The rebellion might have a chance of becoming the revolution."

I need to buy myself some time to clear my head. I don't want anything to happen to my friend, and I need to make sure I don't slip up with my words. "Do you miss living in the sea?"

"Everyone feels the call to the ocean. The longer we stay on land, the stronger it gets."

"What would you do with Maris?" Ryn asks.

"Maybe when she's queen she'll help make merpeople more equal," I say.

"If we bring her here, her father might be persuaded to hand over his power in exchange for her freedom."

I try not to react. My father knows I'm unhappy with how my life's turning out. It's part of the reason we've become so close over such a short time. Maybe that's why he's being so open about this. "You want to kidnap the princess?"

"Don't worry. We wouldn't harm anyone."

I frown. The way I ended up here wasn't exactly conventional. "Am I a prisoner here?" I ask.

"Don't be silly. Of course you're not."

I can't let on that I'm freaking out about what he's just said. "That was silly of me." My laugh comes out fake even to my own ears.

"Surely the princess wouldn't help a human," Ryn says. He's better at acting than me.

"That's what I thought, but you two showing up means it doesn't seem so unlikely."

"What makes you say that?" Ryn asks, keeping his cool.

"Usually, young mer don't come on to land. You never did tell me why you were here."

"Erm..." This was supposed to be breakfast, not an interrogation.

"We're here because we're an unequal match in society and love each other," Ryn says. I guess that fits with us arguing about our relationship last night and is a fraction of the truth. Telling him we've been banished probably wouldn't help the situation, so I nod to agree with him.

"What happened to your mum's job?"

"Mum's always worked at the factory," I say, wondering if that's true. She's always been vague when I've quizzed her about the past. Now I know it's because she hasn't always given me all the details.

"The factory?"

"The shell factory," I clarify.

"What happened to her being a handmaiden at the palace?"

"I must've been too young to remember that." Anger boils within. She never told me she worked with the royals. Is that why she was so against me trying out for the events committee?

"Another wrong that would be put right," my father says.

I nod because I want her to have a second chance, although I don't think I'm willing to pay the price my father's asking for.

"We know Maris, and she'd trust us. Should we head to the beach and see if we can find her?" Ryn asks.

"I already have men out on patrol," my dad says.

"That's good. You seem to be all set."

"How does it work around here?" I ask. "Does everyone have a job?"

This is something I need to know, especially after Ryn's questioning this morning. The food and my father's words are soaking up the alcohol, and I might as well get to the harder stuff before I miss the opportunity.

"Everyone must play their part, Pasha. If you decide

to stay here, that will include you, but as my daughter, your duties will be important."

He sounds like a hypocrite and another male who's going to let me down. I don't want to be the new Maris. I want my own future, not to steal hers. This day is going from bad to worse.

"That sounds intriguing," I say, keeping it vague.

"I'm going to shower before exploring the grounds," Ryn says.

"I could show you around," I offer, pushing my plate away.

"That would be great."

We say goodbye to my dad and practically run back to my room. "Do you think he suspects anything?" I ask.

"We told your father the truth," Ryn says.

I look around. Could my room be bugged? Surely not. Nobody knew I was coming or that Ryn would show up. He gestures to the bathroom, and I turn on the shower. We both strip down and climb in. "Do you think someone's listening in?" I ask.

"I have no idea, but I don't think we should risk it. Let's get our things and take that walk. I noticed the wall near the beachside isn't too high."

"We're going to escape?"

"Unless you've decided you want to stay?"

"No. I'm with you." He kisses me hard on the lips. "I

thought we decided we weren't going to do that anymore."

"You decided that, not me." He leans forward to kiss me but gives me enough time to hesitate. I must be a glutton for punishment because I just can't resist one last touch.

LEO
VIRGO
LIBRA
SCORPIO

Chapter Twenty-One

Aquarians Care About the Planet

Maris

Mermaid laughter and human jealousy seem to be the key ingredients to making the jug give us the next clue. A bead of blue glittery writing appeared after our day at the beach on the inside of the jug pieces. *Mermaids cry tears of joy when sailors shout distress calls of ahoy.*

I'm not sure I would be happy to hear someone's suffering, but I tried to make the pieces fit. It seems me being who I am—a mermaid—and Kasper being who he is—a human—is important to solving the mystery. Actually, I'm beginning to feel like we're fulfilling a prophecy. I've read about them in books but never imagined I could be part of one.

"I think we should go see the oracle," I say to Kasper.

"You spoke of her when we first met, so I'm guessing she lives under the sea. Are you forgetting I'm not a merman? How are you going to explain that?" he asks.

Mermaids aren't fond of humans, and I doubt my father will be understanding.

"We'll avoid everyone but her."

"Do you really think we can do that? And what if she tells your father?"

"If our destiny is to rebuild the Aquarius jug, she won't want to stand in our way."

"Do you think it's fate that brought us together?"

"Don't you?"

"I didn't believe there was a plan for the universe until I met you." He runs his arm down my shoulder, and warmth spreads through me from his touch. I lean in to kiss his lips, wanting to keep hold of this feeling for a little longer.

"Let's go save the world," I say, although I don't want to wake up from this warm, fuzzy feeling.

He frowns but recovers quickly. "Come on, then."

"Wait. What was that look for?"

"It was nothing."

I playfully pout. "I thought you were always real with me."

He rubs his arm then looks into my eyes. "I don't want to, but I'm falling for you, Maris."

Butterflies circle in my stomach. He's the first person to say something like that to me, and the feeling is reciprocated. "I really like you too."

Our lips touch again and we kiss deeper. His tongue massages mine while his hand caresses my cheek. He pulls me close with more need, and it feels like this could be our last intimate moment. We're from different worlds, and that's not going to change, but we have the here and now.

Once we've said goodbye to Owen, we make our way back to the dock near the beach. "Don't look, but I think those two guys are following us," Kasper says.

"Do you think they're the police?"

"They don't seem to be, but I'm not sure who else could be after us. I doubt they'd send a plain-clothed officer to watch over me unless they want to catch me in the act of mischief."

"How are we going to lose them?"

"We'll have to find somewhere to hide until they leave. Two people disappearing into the ocean will look suspicious."

"Should we weave in and out of the crowds until we're out of sight long enough to hide?"

"Yes. I think we should split up, then you slip onto one of the boats as soon as you can. I'll circle back around and catch up with you."

Kasper starts to run, and I take off in a different direction. It quickly becomes apparent he isn't the target. The men are following me, and I have to get away. Pushing myself, I run as fast as I can. A raised stone on the path trips me, and I twist my ankle. Hopping, I try to keep moving forward. Kasper's behind the two guys speeding towards me.

As I approach the end of the dock, my options for escaping are growing slim. I didn't think the ocean was a route I could take, but I have no choice. Leading the men, I make my way to the farthest point of land. Without stopping, I fall into the water and swim down. The men follow me in. They're not human, which means they must be mermen. They don't look familiar, so I doubt they're part of the royal guard. A bad feeling washes over me as I morph into my true form. I need my tail if I'm going to get some distance between us.

I swim as fast as I can towards Atlantis. I'm done with trying to trick them. I need to get onto safe ground. As I reach my city, my own merfolk gather around me.

"Maris, where have you been?" My dad's voice echoes all around me.

"Have the men gone?" I ask, turning to see them swimming away.

My father shouts, "After them!" and chaos breaks out. Mer are everywhere, circling me and chasing after the men. I catch sight of Kasper, who's much slower than everyone else. The guards round him up with the other two, who have already turned into mermen.

"Why have you kidnapped my daughter?" my dad asks.

"If this idiot hadn't tried to stop us, we would've taken her, but we didn't get a chance," one of the guys says, pointing to Kasper.

"Shut up, Rob," the other one says.

"Who are you?" my father asks Kasper.

"Let him go. He's a friend, Daddy," I say.

"Is he the reason you've been missing?"

I pause, knowing this isn't going in my favour.

"Your daughter is a magnificent creature. I'm sorry I've kept her from you, but it was for a good cause."

"Silence!" my dad bellows. "You disobeyed me and left the safety of our city. It was reckless. Do you know what you've put me through? I don't want to hear any more of your stories. Guards, escort her to her room and don't let her out."

"What about Kasper?" I ask.

"The human?" my dad spits out with venom. I nod. "Throw him in the dungeon with the two traitors."

"No!" I say, my voice shaking as tears threaten. "You can't do that."

"You've done enough damage. I'm so disappointed in you."

The guards lead me to my room, where I collapse on the bed. I need to free Kasper and visit the oracle. My father has never listened to me, but he has to this time. It's a matter of life or death, and Owen doesn't have even an hour for us to waste.

"I need to speak to my father urgently," I say, opening the door to the guards. My pulse is racing. I need to stand up for what I believe in and not back down.

"You know he'll come when he's ready," one of them replies.

"That's not going to work for me." I shake my head. I'm not a child anymore and I'm not going to wait for my father to let me out. I swim out of my room and they follow me to the throne. I can hear them muttering their displeasure, but I ignore it.

"We tried to stop her, Your Majesty," a guard says. I roll my eyes.

"Leave us," my dad says, waving them off with a flick of his wrist.

"I'm sorry for disappointing you, but you have to understand I'm old enough to make my own decisions," I tell him.

"Perhaps, Maris, but I need to be able to trust you."

"You can trust me."

"How? I ordered you to stay in your room and you left the kingdom."

It seems like such a long time ago now. "I can't marry Ryn. I'm sorry, but I won't do it. He doesn't love me, and I don't love him."

"You might not think it at the moment, but Ryn is a safe match. He'll look after you and help you run the kingdom."

"Do you know that for sure, or are you judging him on his parents' actions?"

"Something tells me it wouldn't matter which merman I picked out for you. You'd find a flaw."

"When you suggested Ryn as a match, I was willing to give him a chance, but he isn't interested in me. But you're right. I don't think you should be picking me a suitor. I'm capable of choosing my own."

"And what about the human?"

"Kasper's trying to save his brother's life, then they'll

return to England." My father doesn't need to know how deep my feelings for those two run.

"How can I help get him out of here faster?"

"You can let him go. And let us visit the oracle."

"I forbid you from leaving Atlantis," he says in a stern voice.

I may not agree with everything my father wants, but I understand he's worried. "Okay. You have a deal."

He hugs me. "I'm trusting you, Maris. Don't let me down."

"I love you, Daddy."

"I love you too." We hug tightly.

I'm not sure how I'm going to make this work, but I have to stay true to both my father and Kasper.

SCORPIO
LIBRA
VIRGO
LEO

Chapter Twenty-Two

Birthdates between January 20th and February 18th are under Aquarius

Ryn

I'm not willing to throw my heritage away for the rebellion. I need to get out of here fast. After the shower, I dress quickly. Pasha seems to be on board with leaving, but her dad being here changes things.

"Are you ready?" I ask.

"Yes. Let's go for that walk," she says, nodding.

She greets a few mer on our way outside, and I watch her for hesitation. Will she leave with me, or will she change her mind? I've always known she was unhappy with her future, and I would be if we'd been dealt opposite hands. If it was my dad leading these people, would I stand by his side?

Once we reach the back garden wall, we stand, watching the ocean. "Are you sure you want to do this?"

"Are you serious? I may not agree with everything in Atlantis, but I haven't gone insane," she whispers.

"On three I'll give you a leg up?"

"Yes."

"One, two..."

"Neptune, we have a problem," someone shouts, stopping us in our tracks.

We both turn to see where the voice is coming from. "Do you want to find out what's going on?" I ask.

"Do you think it could concern Maris?" A worry line appears on her forehead.

I rub my arm. "I don't know, but it might be useful to find out what they know."

Pasha nods. "Okay. Let's delay."

"I think that's wise."

We head inside to join the others. "It's Rob and Landon. They've been taken by the king's guard."

"Shit," Neptune says, rubbing his head. "Did you see where they went?"

"They were following the princess and she went into the water. I think they've all gone to Atlantis."

"Maris has gone home?" I ask.

I can go home. My smile is uncontrollable as relief fills my body.

"Yes, and the human too."

"Oh, no. This can't be good," Pasha says, unable to hide her concern.

Neptune mistakes her words. "Indeed, it can't, but Rob and Landon are loyal. They won't tell the king anything."

"What are we going to do?" someone asks.

"I could go talk to the king," I say. At least that would get me out of here, and I could ask for the men to be freed.

"What an excellent plan. Now we have you two on our side, we can use it to our advantage."

"Sure," I say. Pasha's eyes are wide, and I kiss her cheek, trying to get her to calm down. "Relax," I whisper.

"Are you up for this, Pasha?" her dad asks.

She slowly nods. "Yes," she says, and it comes out like a squeak. The comfort of a kiss didn't help, so I take more drastic measures by stomping on her foot. "Ouch."

"Sorry," I say, and she fakes a weak smile. She kisses my lips and I take her hand. An understanding passes between us.

"We'll go to Atlantis," Pasha says.

Entering Atlantis after being cast out feels strange. I keep expecting someone to jump out and throw us out, but the place is fairly quiet. Nobody is paying us attention as we enter the palace.

"Is Maris home?" Pasha says as we enter the throne room. I bow to show my respect, and Pasha copies as an afterthought.

"Yes. No thanks to you two," the king says. His voice is laced with anger.

"Thank the starfish," Pasha says, clutching her chest. She doesn't seem concerned by the king's bad mood. "Where is she?"

"She'll be back," the king says. I know him well enough to understand we're not in favour.

My place in the royal court is hopefully restored, but I want to do more to prove this was just a misunderstanding. "We come with news from the rebellion," I say.

"You saw Neptune?" the king asks.

None of the elders has ever admitted anything about the outside world, especially mer on land. "Yes. He seems to think you have some of his mermen."

"That would be correct, but they aren't telling us much."

"We have reason to believe he wants to overturn your leadership," Pasha says.

The king stares at her like she's grown a second head. "Do you know who Neptune is?" he asks curiously.

"He told me he's my father."

"And you haven't formed an alliance?"

"Pardon me for being outspoken, Your Majesty, but I don't want to swap one leader with a vision of inequality for another." She bows her head in respect.

"Your father thought he wasn't given enough powers, and it seems you feel the same way."

"You're mistaken. I don't want to rule anything. I want the opportunity to do a job I could be great at and to marry whoever I like." Pasha speaks with passion.

"Do you mean Ryn?"

"No, but a royal should be able to marry a commoner."

"Or a human?"

That catches us both off guard. This has to be a trick question because the king would never stand for something like that.

"I think what Pasha is trying to say is that she would like a chance to join the events committee."

"This year's annual event was excellent, and Maris did mention your efforts. I'll consider it." He strokes his beard, lost in thought, and I think we've gotten away with having the difficult conversation. "Ryn, my daughter doesn't want to marry you."

I close my eyes as the words sink in. It's not that I want to wed his daughter, but having this conversation makes it more real.

"I'm aware," I say.

"Do you intend to try and fix whatever you did?"

I swallow a gulp of water. I can't believe I'm about to say this to the king and I hope I don't offend him. "No."

He takes a few seconds to consider what I've said, and I hold my breath. "You may both leave," the king says, dismissing us.

We bow and leave the room.

"What now?" I ask.

"I'm going to find Maris. You can do what you want."

What I want to do is return to my home and relax, but instead, I groan. "Okay. Let's go find Maris."

SCORPIO
LIBRA
VIRGO
LEO

Chapter Twenty-Three

The spider is the spirit animal of Aquarius

Kasper

When I envisioned visiting the lost city of Atlantis, I never expected to be spending most of my time behind bars. Fortunately, I was able to persuade the guards to give me my own cell, although listening to my two inmates is the most entertainment I've got.

"How are we going to get out of here?" Rob asks.

"Let's hope Neptune comes for us. It's about time

he set his plan in action to take Atlantis," the other guy says. I heard Rob call him Landon earlier.

"Should we try to escape?" Rob asks.

"This isn't a movie. We can't use a spoon to dig our way out. Besides, even if we weren't sitting on solid rock, it would take months to do something like that."

"Can't we trick one of the guards into letting us out?"

"How do you expect us to do that?" Landon says in a dumb voice. "Your plan is stupid. We might be skeletons before someone comes for us." His annoyance is evident in his voice.

"Your ideas aren't much brighter."

The main door of the prison swings open, and the two men fall silent.

Maris's beautiful face appears at the bars. She's wearing her crown and pearls. Being in the ocean brings her skin to life, and it almost glows. She looks more like a princess than I've ever seen, and it takes my breath away. She's so pretty I'm lost for words.

"Thank the stars you're okay," she says.

"Have you come to get me out, or am I to start begging for an audience with the king?" I ask. Rob has me a little worried I'll be spending the rest of my days down here.

"Of course I've come to get you out," Maris says, waving a key in front of my cell.

"I could kiss you right now." I reach for her, but she doesn't move towards me.

"At least wait until we get outside," she says, playfully tutting. She unlocks the door, and I pull her into a hug. She might be able to wait for a kiss, but I want to touch her.

"What will happen to the other two guys?" I ask, pointing towards their cell as we walk out.

"Aw, did you make prison buddies?" She smirks.

"I'm just curious."

"Princesses don't deal with decisions like that."

"Are you giving me special treatment?" I ask flirtatiously.

"You're my guest. I just needed to sort out the misunderstanding."

"Are you going to show me around?" I gesture to my surroundings, although I hope I won't be seeing any more of these jail walls.

"I think the sea water has gone to your head. We need to get to the oracle and there's no time to waste." We smile at each other. She's right. There's no time to sightsee.

Maris takes my hand to hurry my swimming. We leave the prison and take a route through the city.

"You really care about my brother, don't you?" I ask.

"I do. It feels like I've known him for a lifetime."

"He's a great guy." I smile sadly.

"Yes. I'm looking forward to having some fun with him once we've got the jug."

"And what about with me?"

She pulls me close and gives me the kiss I've been waiting for. "You're cute when you're jealous."

I frown. "That's not what this is."

"Okay. Whatever you say." She's misread me slightly, but I don't correct her. I do wish I could keep her to myself.

We reach a cave that looks like a vintage traveller's shop. Maris runs her fingers through her hair.

"Are you nervous?" I ask, studying her.

"It's been a while since I visited the oracle. She puts me on edge a little."

"Isn't she supposed to help you find your destiny?"

"Yes, but what if I don't want to know what she has to say?"

"Her words don't change fate. It only prepares you for it."

"I hope that's only half true. We need help with our Aquarius clue." Maris pushes forward and enters the dwelling of the oracle.

"Maris, my beautiful child. Please come in," a

mermaid says, gesturing to a seat around a large rock. Her wrinkles highlight her wise age, and her tail isn't as bright as the other mer I've seen.

"Thank you." Maris pulls me farther into the cave and the oracle wastes no time.

She runs her hands over a large black pearl ball. The inside looks like it's moving. I hover in the background, wondering if the mermaid even saw me slip into the room. I've never been a spiritual person, but at this point, I'll try anything. We need to finish solving these clues fast.

"A long time ago, Ganymede was an ordinary boy, minding sheep in his father's field. His masculine beauty attracted the attention of a god. The god of the sky wanted Ganymede for himself. Zeus is said to be the protector of gods and humans, but he also has a mischievous side. He kidnapped the young man from the land using his eagle, who flew him up to the highest heights. The stars of Aquarius represent Ganymede as he became the cupbearer for the gods."

"What does this have to do with us?" Maris asks. She's intensely focused on the oracle.

"Aquarius stars bring good luck, and they are shining down on you. If prophecy prevails, you will restore the heart of Atlantis."

"What about my brother?" I ask.

The oracle makes a crisscross pattern over the pearl, looking deep into the ball. "The jug you seek does contain healing properties, but only fate can decide someone's path."

"What does that mean?" I can't help but worry I'm not going to be able to save Owen, and her words don't fill me with reassurance.

"I can only tell you what I see."

She's not making this easy, but I guess we have to ask the correct question. "We have a riddle to solve relating to the mission. Do you think you can help with unravelling it? It's *mermaids cry tears of joy when sailors shout distress calls of ahoy*," I say, quoting the jug.

She studies her pearl. "Your mind is clouded with the judgement you think is true."

"How do I clear my thoughts?" I've been solely focused on my brother since I arrived in Haiti until I met Maris.

"How did you two meet?"

I frown. What's she trying to say? Maris doesn't cloud my thoughts, does she? "Isn't it your job to already know?" I ask.

"Humour me, dear boy." She looks at me for the first time.

"Maris saved me from drowning."

"So, you were in distress?"

"I was unconscious, but I guess you could call it that."

"And Maris, were you happy to save him?"

"Of course. I wouldn't want anyone to die when I could've been there to rescue them."

"It's more than that, though. You two are soul mates. The stars have aligned to join you together."

"If you think we've already fulfilled the latest clue, where is the piece of the jug?" I ask.

"I cannot be sure, but the signs are showing you need to go back to the location you first met."

"Does the pearl tell you anything else?" Maris asks.

"Only that the waters are looking murky. I want you both to be careful."

"We'll be cautious. Thank you, Oracle," Maris says.

"Yes, thanks," I add.

We did get what we came for. We know where to go. After saying our goodbyes, we head outside. Maris bites her nails.

"What's wrong?" I ask.

"My dad forbids me from leaving the city, and I've already put him through hell." She stops swimming and covers her eyes. "He's going to be so mad."

"This is bigger than you or me. This is about my brother's life. You can't let him down," I say, hoping to talk her around.

"You're right. We'll go back to the place near the treasure box, and I'll come right back. He won't even notice I'm gone."

"I'll look after you, Maris. Everything will be okay."

"We're doing this for Owen. My dad will understand." She nods like she's trying to convince herself. The king seems stubborn, and it's better to ask for forgiveness than waste any more time.

I need her, even if the king will be mad. We can deal with his wrath later. For now, I'm going to put my own wishes first and take the next step to saving my brother.

SCORPIO
LIBRA
VIRGO

Chapter Twenty-Four

Calming blue is Aquarius's spirit colour

Pasha

We're always one step behind Maris, which is the story of my life. The oracle is alone when we arrive, and I don't have to ask her to know we've missed them. Ryn takes one glance at the almost empty room and turns around.

"Come in," the oracle says.

"No. It looks like we've missed the person we came to see," I say, hovering for a few seconds. I'm about to leave when she speaks again.

"Maris and her human have left, but I can offer you a reading," she says.

"I already know how my story turns out. I'll work at the factory until I'm old and grey. No loving husband. No children eating my money away. My cave will be modest but homely. See? There's no need to tell me anything."

"If that's what you want, then you'll make it happen."

I hesitate for a moment, wondering what that means. "Do you see something different?"

"Come sit down."

"I need to find Maris." I point to the door.

"This won't take long, and I may be able to help you find her."

"Okay. I can spare a few minutes." I move to the table, and the oracle casts her hands over her mystical pearl.

"You're at a crossroads. The choices you make in the next few days will affect everything that comes after."

"What should I do?" I don't like that kind of weight on my shoulders. It would be easier if I knew the right answers.

"Only you can decide. Go now or you'll be late."

"Where do I need to be?" My stomach ties up in knots.

"The hidden treasure would be a good starting point." Her eyes glaze over like she's no longer with me. I wait a few seconds, and when she doesn't move, I presume she's done.

"Okay. Thank you."

Ryn's waiting outside when I leave the cave. "What did she say?" he asks.

"We need to go to the shipwreck and locate the treasure box."

"Okay. Let's go." He seems so composed, whereas I'm freaking out inside. I want to be a good person and do the right thing for everyone. I'd rather not be at a crossroads. I'd rather have a straight path to the correct answer.

"I have a bad feeling about this." I bite my lip.

"Did the oracle tell you not to go?"

"No, but she said my decisions will affect my future."

"Do you want to do nothing to influence it?"

He already knows I've been trying to change my job prospects, so his question is a taunt. "I can't do nothing."

"Then what are we waiting for?" He holds out his hand, and I take it.

Maris

As I look up at the choppy water, this feels like déjà vu. The current sweeps up seaweed and driftwood, encircling it around Kasper. My breath hitches as I think of his lifeless body, even though this time I can see his legs kicking.

"How did you get stuck out in the storm?" I ask.

"I met someone who had a book with these coordinates. It said the location has mystical properties that entice sailors. I've been caught out in storms before, but this one tossed me out of my boat like a ragdoll. When I tried to climb back in, the boat capsized, and I found myself gripping onto a piece that had broken off in my hand."

"You were unconscious when I found you."

"It's a good job you did find me. I'm fairly certain I would've drowned if you hadn't."

"Do you remember anything else?"

"Not before you rescued me." He shakes his head. "But I was definitely in distress."

"And I was happy to rescue you." Finding Kasper has changed so much. I'm glad I could save him and get to know him.

"Is that the exact emotion you felt?"

What is he getting at?

"Exposing ourselves to humans is frowned upon, so I hesitated, but I knew what I had to do."

"Why didn't you take me to the land?"

"With the water being so rough, I'd have had to leave the water to ensure you were safe, and I was worried I would be seen."

"Did you see any lights or shooting stars? Anything that could've symbolised where the jug was?"

"I'd have told you if I had. We should look around." Beneath the water, the shipwreck and caves lie along with the treasure chest I found many months ago. We search the whole area, leaving no corner unturned.

"Do you think the oracle could've been mistaken about the clue?" Kasper asks.

"No. She doesn't make mistakes, but that doesn't mean she told us the whole truth. We're obviously missing something."

"We never had a near miss or an actual kiss here. Do you think that could be it?" he asks while we both feel along the cave wall.

"Exploring the cave with you isn't romantic, and forcing kisses is a turn-off."

"I'm not sure those were your thoughts in Brazil."

My face heats with embarrassment at how turned on

I was that night. Kasper was the perfect gentleman, and this is the first time he's mentioned how I reacted to him. "It's a beautiful place and easy to become lost in."

He moves closer to me. "And you're beautiful too. I could get lost in you." He strokes my hair.

"Okay, I take it back. You can change my mood at the flick of a switch."

He sinks back into the pool and captures my lips. I can't help the soft moan as his hard chest brushes close to mine. A tingle starts in my core, and my tail transforms into legs.

"I thought you didn't want to get out of the water?" Kasper asks.

"I don't. Or I didn't."

He gives me a puzzled look, and I'm back to feeling embarrassed. "Please don't make me spell it out."

He narrows his eyes. "What?"

My tail shimmers back into place. "Are you only doing this for the jug?" I ask.

"Doing what?"

"Kissing me." I frown, hoping his feelings run deeper.

"You mean more to me than any woman I've ever met."

I smile. "Do you think we would've dated if we'd met through different circumstances?"

"From the moment I met you, I knew you were special. Not because you saved me or because you're a mermaid. It's because of what's in here." He touches my chest over my heart.

My pulse quickens and butterflies jumble in my stomach. "I'm not sure what this feeling is, but I've never felt like this either."

He runs his tongue over my bottom lip. Lust fills me, and I struggle to hide it. My own tongue darts out to wet my dry mouth. It softly meets his, and he pulls me into a toe-curling kiss, our hands exploring each other's bodies. My tail disappears once more, and he slips his hands over my ass.

"I think I'm beginning to understand what's happening." He massages the top of my leg.

"I'm sorry," I say.

"Being turned on is nothing to be embarrassed about." He guides my hand towards his erection, and I gasp. It's the first time I've felt a dick, and it's hard under his underwear. He encourages me to wrap my fingers around his length, and I give it a little squeeze.

"You want me too?" I say, but it comes out more like a question.

"Every time we kiss, but it doesn't have to mean anything more than what we have."

"What if I want it to mean more?" I don't really

know what I'm asking for. We have no future, but we have now.

"Are you trying to lead me astray, princess?"

"Do you want me to stop?" I ask, stroking him through his boxers.

"Don't you dare."

I smile against his mouth, happy I have this effect on him. His hand moves further between my legs, and my folds slicken in anticipation. He cups my mound right as a loud crash brings us back to the present. We're no longer alone, but my back is to our intruder. Whoever it is, I can't imagine this ending well for us. My father won't be happy I've been caught in a compromising position with a human.

SCORPIO
LIBRA
VIRGO
LEO

Chapter Twenty-Five

Aquarians like to stand out from the crowd as individuals

Ryn

When we started to follow Neptune, I never thought I'd be seeing Maris naked for the first time with a human pawing all over her. I've always taken the future we had planned out for granted. Now it's slipping away, I kind of feel sad. Not because I have feelings for Maris. I don't. It's selfish, but being king meant my life was set. What am I going to do without that? The king would never let Maris marry a human, but this changes things. She'd never let me touch her like that because she said she was waiting for her husband.

Maris's tail shimmers back into place as Pasha gasps.

"What are you doing here?" Maris asks. Her face is crimson as she swims in front of Kasper to cover his erection.

"We're here to find you, but Pasha's dad might have his own motive," I say.

"Princess, you're going to help me get my mermen back and get an audience with the king," Neptune says, and my already queasy stomach takes a bigger dive. I feel trouble is brewing, and I'm going to be dragged into it.

Maris is looking at me, and she must see something in my frown that makes her cautious. "Your men were chasing me when I was on land. What if I refuse to help you free them?" Maris asks.

"You have no choice. You're outnumbered," Neptune says, and I'm pretty sure he's including me and Pasha in his headcount of allies. I have to wait for the right time to reveal whose side I'm on.

"You'll let my friend go. He's of no concern to you," Maris says, gesturing to Kasper.

"You're in no place to make demands, but I'll allow it." Neptune gestures for Maris to lead the way out of the cave.

I grab hold of Pasha's hand so she's forced to look at me.

"The oracle said my decision today would be significant," she says, following them out into the open sea.

"What does that mean?" I ask, but she doesn't get a chance to respond.

"Pasha, I want you up here with me," Neptune says.

Her hand untangles from mine and she gives me a look I can't decipher. My heart pounds in my chest. Would she betray her fellow mermaids for her father?

I slip to the back of the group, and when I think I'm forgotten about, I go back to get Kasper. Never in my life did I think I'd need the help of a human. Once back in the cave, I find him holding a piece of what I think is the Aquarius jug. "Have you only found one piece so far?"

"No. The rest is in a safe location. This is the latest one. Do you think they'll harm Maris?"

"I don't really know the man that's taken her, but I think he intends to hurt the king."

"And what are we going to do about it?"

"The only upper hand we have is that we already know what they want. It'll no longer be a surprise to us when they enter Atlantis. You're the one who's good at following clues. What do you suggest?"

"What will Pasha's other family think of this?"

"I doubt her mum will be on board. The woman seems

like a hard-ass from the times I've met her, and she obviously isn't with her dad. I know where she lives, so going there is probably the best idea we've got. Let's go." I turn to leave.

"Wait."

"What?"

"I'm human and not a fast swimmer. I'm going to need some help getting there."

"You were getting frisky with my fiancée, and now you want to hold my hand? Anyone would think you had a thing for merfolk," I tease.

"She's too good for someone like you."

I grit my teeth, but I can't disagree. "You don't know anything about me."

"That's where you're wrong. I've seen the effect you've had on Maris, and I don't like it. Both of those girls deserve someone who can give them everything."

"So, the human's really a saint," I mutter, holding out my hand for him to take.

"I've made asshole decisions, and I'm not proud of some of the things I've done, but I love Maris and want what's best for her."

He grabs hold of me and pulls himself close. We're chest to chest. "Chill out, Romeo. The person who's going to stand in your way isn't me. The guy you need to worry about is the king."

"I know we don't have a future, but I'd like to think she'll find someone worthy."

"Excellent, but right now we have a city to save, so let's go."

I help him secure a good hiding spot for his piece of the broken jug before we swim to Pasha's house. I squeeze his hand harder than necessary, but it makes me feel better about him judging me. I'm used to people either looking up to me or being envious. Kasper doesn't do either of these things, which shouldn't bother me, but it does.

When Pasha's mum catches sight of us, she ushers us inside. "Why have you brought a human to my dwelling?" she scolds.

"That's the least of our worries," I say.

"Then what are you doing here?"

"Neptune's captured Princess Maris and is going to use her as leverage."

"My ex-husband?" She rubs her hands over her face in disbelief.

"Yes."

"Where is he, and where is my daughter?"

"They're probably heading to the prison, then the throne room. Or maybe just the throne room."

"Pasha's with her father?"

"I'm afraid so, although I have no idea whose side she's on."

"How could you let this happen and what does it have to do with this human?"

"The human belongs to Maris."

"I have a name," Kasper says, holding out his hand. Pasha's mum looks at it but doesn't accept it straight away. "I'm Kasper. I don't mean anyone any harm, but I'd like to get on with rescuing Atlantis so I can finish my mission."

"The last time I met a human was the day my Neptune let out his wrath on the city. You can call me Angel."

"I never said I was a good luck charm, but I'm here to help," Kasper says.

"I'm Ryn," I say, because I've never formally been introduced to Pasha's mum.

"I know who you are," Angel says, not looking too happy about it.

"Okay, now that's all sorted, shall we go?" Kasper says, making my lips crack into a smile. He's so matter-of-fact and nothing like me.

We all agree it's time to head to the castle, and once I have a hold of Kasper's hand, I lead the way. We don't look like the perfect team of heroes, but we'll have to do.

SCORPIO
LIBRA
VIRGO

Chapter Twenty-Six

Aquarius is a Forgiving Star Sign

Pasha

My head is spinning from the turn of events. I'm pretty certain I'm in big trouble, and the oracle's words are weighing heavily on my mind. It's so important I get this right. If I don't, Atlantis will be doomed, or at the very least, I will be.

My father holds his posture firm as he enters the castle. Maris is by my side, but I dare not glance at her. I wonder what she's thinking? Does she hate me more than she already did?

"That's my throne, Cyrus. Now, move," Neptune says.

One of my dad's men holds a dagger to Maris's throat, and I have to fight the urge to swim towards her. She lets out a gasp, and I squeeze my fist into a ball.

"What are you doing here?" the king asks. His eyes widen, even though Ryn and I warned him this might be coming. Threatening his daughter is a low blow.

"Guards, go get my men," my dad says. The guy with the dagger tightens his grip on Maris.

"Hold it," the king says. "Will someone please tell me what's going on?"

He moves forward but stops when Maris lets out a squeal. "You're hurting me," she says.

"Your reign as king is over." My dad holds a dagger up towards the king.

"How did you work that out? This is my kingdom. It was sixteen years ago, and it still is now. You're the outcast."

"We have your daughter and an army outside the city waiting for my signal."

"Why now?" The king signals for one of his guards to look outside. He moves towards the door and my dad waves the dagger towards him. The guy holds his hands up and slowly swims out of the room.

"This has been a long time in the making. When I

realised your daughter might be outside Atlantis, I knew we had to try our luck. Not everyone supported your ruling sixteen years ago, and not everyone does now. The difference is, I'm in a stronger position now."

The king's guard returns, "He has men outside."

If the king had listened to us, he'd have his own army ready.

One of my dad's guards leaves the room and, using force, a few men help my dad remove the king from his chair. He struggles but he's outnumbered as more guys swim into the room. Two other guards I've never seen before take the king away.

My insides are jumbled with nerves. The guards gesture me and my friends over to some seats. The guy with the dagger moves away from Maris. All we can do is sit and watch while the nightmare unfolds before our eyes.

Merfolk pledge their loyalty to my father like they've been waiting for this day to arrive. I can't work out if they're scared or actually loyal. I knew nothing of my father until I went on land because not even my mother told me the truth. The whole thing makes me feel like I've missed something. These mer never once offered me a helping hand for being my father's daughter, and now he's in power, they're all looking at me differently. The oracle said my actions would change everything, but that doesn't help me figure out what to do.

I'm biting my nails away by the time my mother turns up. "Neptune, this is ridiculous. Why have you come here? You're not wanted!" she shouts.

"You were always short-sighted. I had to wait for the time to be right before I returned. Change is needed, and that's what I'm offering. There will be no more royals. Instead, there will be a leader, me, and everyone else will be treated equally."

"Why now?" She crosses her arms.

"I waited too long to make this day a reality, but I have Maris now. The king won't want anything to happen to his only daughter."

"What about the mer against you?"

"This is the uprising. We've stayed quiet for too long. If you're not with me, then you can have the caves on the outskirts of the city. Atlantis will be glorious once more."

"Come on, Pasha and Maris, we're leaving," my mum says.

"You have no power in here," my dad says.

I look between them before getting up. "Do I have to stay here? Is Maris your prisoner?"

My father studies me, but I don't know what he's trying to work out. "You're free to do what you want," he says, but his tone makes me think it could be a test rather than the truth.

I'm poised, ready to move while I wait to find out what I should do. Maris swims to be with my mother, and nobody tries to stop her. "Will you let them leave?" I ask my dad.

"I've already got what I want from the princess. Maris will be stripped of her status and shamed for mating with a human. She isn't worthy of the crown, so she is free to leave with your mother."

"And what about me?" I study his face as he studies mine.

"You've always shown promise, Pasha. If you stay with me, one day, all this will be yours." He waves his arms wide, offering me things that don't belong to him.

"This is a lot to take in. I'd like to get some air," I say.

I'm wary of trusting him, and I need to get out of here. I need to talk to my family and friends. Without looking back, I swim out of the throne room, heading for the surface. It takes a while for the others to join me, and I'm a nervous wreck by the time they show up.

Kasper and Maris surface first.

"What took you so long?" I ask.

"We needed to regroup and get the jug," Maris says.

"Is it complete?"

"There's only one piece left to get," Kasper replies, showing me a piece of broken pottery.

Ryn's next to join us, and my mother isn't far behind him. "Are you planning on going back in there?" Ryn asks.

"I didn't know what was best to do. He seems to trust me, so maybe I should stay and keep an eye on the situation."

"I think I should come with you," Ryn says. I need to completely break things off him, but I don't want to go back in there on my own. I'll talk to him once we're alone.

"What are you two going to do?" I ask Maris and Kasper.

"We need to go after the last piece of the jug," Kasper says.

"Yes. The oracle said it was key," Maris adds.

"Okay. I wish you luck," I say. Maris hugs me. There's so much I want to say to her and catch up with, but now is not the time. "What about you, Mum?" I ask.

"I'm going to see if I can round up the mer who are loyal to the king."

"How do you know who they are?"

"The royals and the ones who were not pleased when Neptune escaped the first time will be a good starting point."

"Okay. Be careful," I say, hugging her.

"You too." She wraps her arms around me tightly. "Don't underestimate your father. It's likely he's questioning your loyalty."

"I'll try to shake his suspicion."

We say our goodbyes, and I move closer to Ryn. I'm going to need his support to get through this, and my dad already thinks we're a couple. I shouldn't give him mixed signals about our relationship, but I can't do this alone. I've got to try and act natural around my father, and I can't explore the complexity of our relationship right now. Ryn and I join hands as we make our way back inside. The small connection already makes me feel better about handling this situation.

"Where have you been?" my dad asks.

"I'm worried about Mum. I expected her to be happy to see you," I say.

"It's a shame she's not joining us. Where did your boyfriend go when we left the cave? He seems to have a lot of human friends," he says, addressing me instead of Ryn. Does he know Ryn went back to the cave for Kasper, or is he testing our loyalty?

Ryn cuts me off before the first word is out of my mouth. "I can answer for myself. Isaac, the guy from land, is a tradesman, not a friend. He helped me find Pasha and I had to pay for his help. Kasper is Maris's human and of no significance to me," Ryn says, sounding bored. He seems to be good at keeping his head clear under pressure.

My dad seems to accept our answers. Over the next hour, we get a glimpse into how deep the uprising goes. If I said I wasn't worried, I'd be lying. I hope Maris knows what she's doing by going after the jug instead of trying to take back power.

Pretending to be loyal to my father might not be what the oracle had in mind, but this is the decision I've made, and I try my hardest to be believable. The royals are cleared out of the castle, and my father says I can have any room I like. We spend the night in Ryn's quarters.

"Are you okay?" he asks once we're alone.

"Not really. What about you?" I ask.

"We're together, so we'll work it out." He softly kisses my lips. It's caring and relaxing, unlike the other ones we've shared. He caresses my shoulders and pulls me close. "I've got you, Pasha, and this time I'm not letting you go."

He kisses me again, and I take the comfort he's offering. I need support now more than ever. Ryn's never been there for me, but now I really need it, he's here, and it feels good.

SCORPIO
LIBRA
VIRGO
LEO

Chapter Twenty-Seven

Four is a Lucky Number for Aquarius

Maris

My world is crumbling around me, and all I can do to help is keep looking for the last piece of the jug. It doesn't feel like enough. I want to kick Neptune out of my dad's chair and put the rightful king back on his throne, but I feel helpless. I don't know which merfolk are on my side and who are traitors. Is this why my dad always tried to keep me around the royals? I understand why he didn't like Pasha now.

I've never been in a situation where I'm the one

making the big decisions, and I'm going to need as many allies as I can find. First, I must stay true to my word and help find the jug. Kasper and I have come so far, and we can't delay our mission. Owen's counting on us, and he can't wait for me to save my city. Everything is a mess.

"Are you okay?" Kasper asks once we're alone. He must have noticed I'd zoned out.

"How am I going to save Atlantis?" I ask, biting my lip.

"One of the things I've learnt from this experience is that we should look at each piece of a situation individually. It was a mammoth task to get this far, but we got through it by keeping our focus. We've been to Brazil, Dominican Republic, and back to Haiti. We literally crossed lands and oceans to bring the jug together. I couldn't have done this without you." He kisses me softly.

I cover my face when memories of the last time we were intimate flash through my mind. "I can't believe I got caught naked with you." My face is burning with embarrassment.

"I can't believe we got interrupted. We have some making up to do." He slips his arm around my butt. The piece of jug is still in his hand.

"I'm being serious. My innocent reputation is ruined."

Kasper has a way of lightening the situation, and I find myself laughing at my indiscretion. Before I met him, I wouldn't have considered doing something that shines a bad light on me. Now, I feel like a vixen, but it's all for him. Kasper makes me feel like nobody ever has.

"With a human too. It's scandalous." He laughs playfully, and I can't help but smile.

"Hopefully, Pasha and Ryn won't tell my dad."

"Are you ashamed of me?" he asks with a frown.

I shake my head. "No. It's just my dad and the merfolk might not be accepting of you."

"If I help you save Atlantis, maybe they'll see it differently." He rubs my arm, and I circle his wrist with my thumb.

I like his optimism.

"I hope you're right." It would be nice if my dad became more accepting of change. I've seen how Pasha has struggled with not having the right connections, and I thought being her friend was enough. Now I can see she's not the only one who would like a fairer chance in Atlantis, but I'm getting ahead of myself. "Have you had a chance to study our latest clue?"

He holds the jug up to the light so he can read the inscription. "The moon shines brightest when love is in the air."

"It doesn't give us much to go on. Other than having to wait until it gets dark," I say, thinking out loud.

"And don't forget, we have to bring the romance." Kasper winks at me.

"I hope we'll be able to avoid an audience this time."

He nods. "That would be great. I'd like to get rid of my blue balls."

I playfully swat his arm, but I feel a little flushed. He's messing with me, but I've felt his arousal when we've been kissing. "You're wicked."

He laughs. "If you're lucky, I'll show you how naughty I can be later."

I fan my face. "I look forward to it."

Our attraction is more than being thrown together for the stars. I really care about him and want to get closer to him.

"Come on. Let's get a move on before we get caught doing something else we shouldn't be. Let's go on land so we can check on Owen and gather the rest of the pieces."

"Yes, that sounds like a good idea." I'm disappointed he doesn't want to kiss some more, but he's right. It's the middle of the day, and we're a mermaid and a human in the middle of the ocean. If a boat found us, we'd have some explaining to do, even if I transformed my tail.

Thinking back to the clue, I ask, "Do you think the

moon shines brightest at a certain time?" We swim towards the land, keeping out of sight.

"I don't have a clue, but we'll find out."

"What is a supermoon?" I ask.

"It's the answer to your question. The moon is brightest when it's closest to Earth," Owen says, and Kasper leans over his shoulder to read the same book.

"Okay, so when's the next one?" Goosebumps pucker over my skin. We are so close to having the whole jug.

They both flick through books to try and find the answer. "It seems to be different every year. We need to find a computer so we can access the internet," Kasper says.

"Shall we go to the library?" I ask.

"Yes. Let me grab my jacket."

"Me too," Owen says, making his brother pause.

"You should stay here," Kasper says.

"I'm feeling fine and I want to come." Owen glares at his brother.

Kasper hesitates, ready to argue, but then he shakes his head. "Okay."

Owen's smile beams across his face. For the first time since we met, he looks determined to succeed. Once we're ready, we walk to the library and find a computer.

"I can't believe our luck," I say.

"What does it say?" Owen asks.

"The next supermoon is tonight." I clap giddily.

Kasper holds his cheeks, pulling his skin back towards his scalp. "It's almost over." A sob leaves his lips, and the three of us huddle. Emotions are running high, and it gives me a buzz. I'm so happy to have met these two amazing humans, and I feel the sentimental bond deepen between us.

"I want to come with you guys," Owen says.

"It usually gets romantic between us when we see the stars," Kasper says, trying to lighten the mood as well as warn his brother.

"I knew there was something between you two." Owen smiles.

"You should still come tonight. It will be nice to have you and the jug ready to go," I say.

"Where are you going? Do you have a location?"

"There was no location mentioned in the clue, but I'm guessing we need to be close to the ocean," Kasper says.

"And the land," I add.

"And the stars," Kasper says with a smile. Our eyes meet, and I smile.

"Maybe love is in the air," Owen says, breaking the trance we're in.

"We've only known each other a few weeks," Kasper says.

"It couldn't be love," I say, shaking my head.

I've already rushed my feelings with one man. I won't make the same mistake again. Kasper is nothing like Ryn, and he seems to only have eyes for me, but we don't know each other well enough for it to be love, right? Plus, I'm a mermaid and he's a human. We live in completely different surroundings. My dad won't accept him, and I don't want to leave Atlantis.

I shake my head. "No. It can't be love."

SCORPIO
LIBRA
VIRGO

Chapter Twenty-Eight

Aquarians are Water-Loving

Ryn

It would be so much easier if our every move wasn't being watched. I have a chance to spend real time with Pasha, but the guards are cramping my style. I lie on one of the lounge chairs, trying not to doze off. If I thought life was a little dull before the king was overthrown, it definitely is now. All the staff have been sent home to pursue their dreams, which means the food's not being cooked, the pillows aren't getting replenished, and the place looks like a wild animal ransacked it. There are even piles of fish bones left on the floor. "Do you think we should go out for a swim?" I ask Pasha, needing to get out of here.

She looks up from her book. "I was hoping to finish this chapter."

"You can read anytime. It's not like there's much else to do around here."

"I'm enjoying the freedom. Usually, I'd have chores to do, and my mum wants me to get a job at the shell factory." She touches the book to find her place.

"Some jobs are supposed to be done. Look at the state of this throne room. You can't honestly be enjoying this." I wave towards the empty plates and fish bones.

"If you're so bothered by the mess, why don't you clean it up?" She forcefully throws down the book.

"I didn't make it." I shake my head.

"No, that's right. You've lived a privileged life."

"Why are you trying to fall out with me? All I asked was if you wanted to go for a walk."

"I'm sorry. I guess I'm just worried. Maybe we should go for that walk." She looks at the guards.

When we step outside, they don't follow us, and I'm relieved. "It's intense in there," I say, rubbing my head.

"You're right, it is intense in there, but when it's all over, we're going to be apart, and I'm sick of pretending with us. One minute we're pretending we're not in love, and now we're pretending we are. I don't want to do it anymore, Ryn."

"The king has freed me from my engagement to Maris. I can date who I like."

"I never understood why the king disliked me so much, but now I do. It doesn't change the fact you're a royal and I'm not, though. My father has put the king in jail, so I doubt he'll accept us as mates. The only way this ends for me is badly. I won't be welcome in the royal court if my father's overturned, and I dread to think what will happen if he's not."

"You're going to help fix the problem. The king will see you're nothing like your father."

"Is that true, though?"

"What do you mean?"

"I don't want to see lesser merfolk have to slave over the king."

"Have you ever thought that the people who serve the king do it because they see they're doing something they can be proud of?"

"Do you truly believe that?"

"You don't have to take my word for it. I can prove it." I've talked to the staff before, and I consider some of them my friends. One mermaid comes to mind who I don't think would mind me calling on her.

"Okay. Let's see it, then."

"First, I think we should circle the square to make sure we're not being followed."

"Did you not see the guard hiding behind the clam statue, pretending to read the newspaper?"

"Damn it. You should've told me. I would've been more careful with my words."

"He probably thinks we're just having a spat."

"Shall we split up?"

"No. I have a better idea. We'll disappear under a coral patch and he'll think we're making out or something. Then we'll sneak out of the back and make a getaway."

We do as Pasha suggests, and the guard stays reading his paper but keeps glancing in our direction. At first, we stay just in sight so he can see we're getting close to each other.

"I want to apologise for making you feel second class. It wasn't my intention to make you feel like you weren't good enough for me," I say.

"If that's not what you think, why did you tell Maris I don't mean anything to you?"

"Because I wanted to be king. Now I can see that was stupid. Maris is nice, but she's not for me."

"If my dad stays in power, maybe one day you could still be king."

"No. That's not my future." I've never been sure of

much, but I know I'm too selfish to rule a whole city of people.

"What do you want?"

"All I can tell you is that I love you."

She rolls her eyes. "I wish you'd stop saying stuff like that. It's hollow if it isn't going to lead to anything."

"I haven't got it all figured out yet, but when I do, I'm going to show you how wrong you are." I didn't expect the first time I told someone I loved them I'd get rejected. She isn't saying she doesn't feel the same way, but it feels like she is.

"The guard is distracted. We should make a run for it now," Pasha says and swims behind the coral. She doesn't wait for me as she speeds off, and I have to push hard to catch up with her. When we're certain we've got away, I show her the way to Starlyn's cave.

"Hello," I shout as we swim inside. The amount of merfolk crammed into this small space gives me pause. "What's going on?" I ask.

"That's Neptune's daughter," someone says, and all eyes turn to us so they can glare.

Pasha holds her hands up. "I don't mean you any harm. Tell them, Oracle."

The mermaid in question steps forward from the shadows to study her. "I can see your mother in you, but there's also a darkness from your father."

"We came to talk to Starlyn about her job in the palace. Is she happy to clean for the king, or does she do it because she has to?" Pasha asks. She's looking at the oracle, even though she's really asking her question to Starlyn.

"Is that what you think, dear?" the mermaid I assume is Starlyn asks as she swims forward.

"I really want to do something more than work at the shell factory, but my mum has always said it wasn't possible," Pasha says.

"That's because the king punished her for your dad rebelling the first time."

"My mum didn't do anything wrong."

"How many times have I said that?" Fishkiss—another helper at the palace—says.

The crowd erupts into speaking their minds. "Silence," the oracle says. "We will all find our true place in this world. You will too, Pasha."

"I'm not unhappy working for the king. In fact, I've enjoyed watching the royals grow up as I don't have any family of my own," Starlyn says.

"Thank you for being honest with me," Pasha says.

"Your mother's a good woman, and the king should've seen that."

"Thank you. It means a lot that you say that."

"Seeing you here is significant, but you can't know too much about our plans," the oracle says.

"I trust you," Pasha tells her.

"Is there anything we can do?" I ask.

"When we give the signal, be ready. For now, return to the palace and stay under the radar," the oracle says.

"We will do," I say, and we leave.

Pasha seems lost in thought as we return home.

LEO
VIRGO
LIBRA
SCORPIO

Chapter Twenty-Nine

Aquarians are most happy when they help others

Maris

The campfire glows amber as the dark sky begins to twinkle with stars. I feel at peace as I sit between my two favourite men.

"So, what happens now?" Owen asks.

"We wish to the Greek gods that we're in the right place," I say.

"And usually there's some kissing."

"Well, don't let me stop you," Owen says, resting back on his hands and looking up at the stars.

It's a little awkward at first, but we soon get into it.

About an hour later, we both roll onto our backs. "My jaw's aching, and I don't think that's working."

"Charming," Kasper says, laughing.

"There you go, brother. You've blown it," Owen jokes.

"We're obviously missing something," I say.

"Our make-out sessions have been intense lately." Kasper winks.

"I don't think that's it," Owen says.

"Come on, then. You've not been there to solve any of the other clues, but let's hear you steamroll in and claim this one."

"Actually, I'm not claiming anything, but I'm willing to admit I love Maris. Obviously in a sisterly way, but nonetheless, Maris, I think you're incredible for everything you've done, and I love you."

"Aw, thank you, Owen. I love you too."

"Should we have a little kiss now?" he asks, making me chuckle. He's so sweet, and I'm honoured to be thought of so highly.

"Let's do it." I sit up and he does the same. He leans in to kiss my cheek, but I turn my head. Close friends can kiss on the lips and it can still be platonic. We share a quick peck, and my heart swells. I never thought I'd love a human in any way, never mind two, but these guys mean everything to me.

"That was cute," Kasper says.

"Yes, it was. Owen might be my favourite now," I joke.

"You wound me. I'm not sure my heart can take that." Kasper clutches his chest.

"But I still love your friendship too," I say.

"Burn," Owen says.

"Oh, shut it," Kasper says, laughing. "I love you also, Maris, but it isn't like a sibling."

Owen laughs loudly, making himself cough. Kasper and I freeze.

"Maris is beautiful and kind. She deserves more than a half-assed love confession," Owen says.

"Thanks, Owen, and one day, I'll get one from my future husband."

"He's one lucky merman." We're lost in our conversation when Kasper starts to shush us. "What?" Owen asks.

"Look over there." He points to the sky where a cluster of stars has started to get brighter. The outline of a mermaid appears made out of something like the northern lights, and she comes to life like a cartoon. We're all mesmerised by her.

"We have a mermaid, but who will she fall in love with?" Owen asks.

The cartoon begins to cry, and tiny stars shoot down her face like fireworks.

I scope around, looking for her lover. She can't be sad and alone because that's not how this story has been going. The jug of Aquarius comes to life next, and the man who carries it. I think this might be Ganymede because he's the owner of the jug in Greek mythology. He catches the mermaid's tears until she stops crying. Even though Ganymede was taken by Zeus, did he find his soulmate amongst the stars? The mermaid and the man kiss, and shooting stars fly over their picture until it blurs away. Owen's holding the last piece of the jug once the image in the sky disappears.

"Wow. That was amazing," Owen says.

"Yes. We can finally put this together." Kasper picks up the other bits.

"Do you think it will glue itself together?" I ask.

"There's only one way to find out."

We lay the pieces out and try to fit them together.

"You've been across land and sea. I bet a little bit of ocean water and sand might help," Owen says.

"It's worth a shot," Kasper agrees.

We scoop up wet sand close to the sea and use it to hold the jug together. The blue obsidian starts to glow and runs into the cracks of the pieces.

"It's working," I say. I'm filled with excitement.

The jug lifts into the air, spinning on an axis. Sand grains, water from the sea, and light from the stars all circulate like magic around us. Once the jug solidifies, it moves towards me and rests in my hands. It's like it's chosen me as the new keeper, even though I'm not the one who needs it. Or at least, I don't think I am.

Owen leans over me to inspect the contents. "It's empty. What do we fill it with? Ocean water?"

"Mermaid tears," Kasper says. We both look to him. "The jug chose you. It makes sense your essence makes it work."

A sense of pride washes over me. Finding the jug has been amazing, but to know I'll be the one to make the magic work is special. "This feels unreal, and I'm so happy we did it." I fill up with emotions and tears spill down my cheeks. Kasper and Owen kiss my face, making me smile. "I want to save you, Owen."

"I never thought it was possible. When Kasper brought you home, I knew you would change everything," Owen says.

Kasper runs his finger over my happy tears and picks them up. He runs his hand over the rim of the jug, and it rings, almost like a glass filled with water. The inside fills with blue sparkly liquid. I pass the jug to Owen, and he drinks from it. The blue of his eyes brightens as he sweeps up into the air. The magic spins him around and light beams out of his hands and feet. When he comes back down to Earth, his skin looks healthier, his muscles are tighter, and his hair looks silky smooth.

"Wow. How do you feel?" I ask.

"Like a new man," Owen says. The joy on his face gives me a buzz.

"You look like one too."

"Hey, stop ogling my brother," Kasper says.

"He looks good." I smile.

"He does."

"Thank you. Both of you. I owe you my life," Owen says. His voice shakes as he struggles to get his words out. A happy tear slides down his face.

"What are you going to do now?" I ask.

"I'm going back to England, and I'm going to live my life to the fullest. I want to get married and buy a big house. I want to earn an honest living."

"You've got to find someone who will have you first," Kasper says, laughing, and Owen rolls his eyes.

I love seeing them like this. The sadness between them brought them down, and now it's lifted. It's amazing to think I was part of that.

"I'm going to sweep some unexpecting person off their feet," Owen says.

"Aw, that's sweet," I say.

"What about you, Maris? What are you going to do?"

"I'm going to save Atlantis," I say, feeling empowered by that idea.

"You're not going to marry Ryn, are you?" Kasper asks.

"No. I will only marry for love."

"Good for you," Owen says.

"Do you want us to help you save Atlantis?" Kasper asks.

"I have the jug and some merfolk on my side. My species will not accept you, and I don't want to complicate things. I think you should go back to England and I'll lead my folk."

"You've got this, Maris," Owen says. He hugs me and kisses my cheek. "I'll give you two some space to say goodbye. Thanks for everything." I squeeze him tightly and we say our farewells.

"So," Kasper starts. "I'm going to miss you."

"Me too. My favourite human."

"I love you. I mean that." He leans in and captures my lips. We kiss with passion, but it also feels like a goodbye.

"I love you too," I say when we break apart.

"Good luck with Atlantis."

"Thanks. I'm going to take back what's mine, just like Owen has."

We kiss and cuddle a few more times. I've enjoyed our mission, but I'm ready to return home. I'd love to see the guys building their lives back up, but I'm a mermaid, and returning to the sea is what's right.

SCORPIO
LIBRA
VIRGO
LEO

Chapter Thirty

Air signs like Gemini and Libra are good companions for Aquarius

Pasha

"Renounce the throne, Cyrus, and this will be all over," my father shouts as electric eels make contact with the king's torso. He lets out a scream of pain but doesn't say anything. "Again," my dad says, and they slither around to approach their victim.

"Is this necessary?" I ask. I've never seen anyone be tortured before, and I wouldn't wish this on my mortal enemy.

"Are you questioning my judgement?" My father turns to look at me.

"This is intense to watch."

"Then leave." He turns his back and waves his hands towards the eels to signal they should carry on. I swim forward, but Ryn grabs hold of me, shaking his head as a warning.

"We can't do nothing," I whisper.

"Remember your loyalty," Ryn says. He doesn't mean to my father. He's trying to make me see the consequences of my actions. I stop fighting him and relax into him for support.

"Let's take a swim," I say.

We almost make the door when my father speaks. "If you can't stomach this, maybe you should have a long, hard think before you come back."

The oracle warned me he would test me. I just hadn't realised how brutal it would be.

Changing direction, I avoid Ryn's protest and swim right up to my father. "Is hurting people what you like to do?" I ask.

"Only when I have to," my dad says. His expression tightens into a grimace.

"You could literally take his crown off his head and put it on your own."

"The throne wouldn't truly be mine then."

"It won't be if you get him to agree under false pretences either."

"Then what do you suggest? I want the throne. I'm the rightful king. How do you think I should get it?"

"If the merfolk want you to rule, then you will be in charge."

"If only it was that simple. Once the crown truly belongs to me, it won't matter who the merfolk want. They'll have me. Again!" He shouts the last part, and the eels do their thing. I'm so close I can smell the electrical current burning its victim. I fight not to shudder, but it's hard as an overwhelming distaste for my father sinks in. How can the oracle question my loyalty? There is no choice to be made here, and I can't support this evil man.

A loud horn stops me from making my move as angler fish flood into the room. The throne room plummets into darkness, except for the last lash of the electric eels. I involuntarily flinch away from them. The sharp teeth of the angler fish could easily rip through my skin, never mind the threat behind me. My heart feels like it's going to jump out of my chest as it beats erratically. I'm light-headed, but I must stay focused. The fishes' bioluminescent rods light up, and the pretty but deadly animals circulate the room. The screams that follow send shudders down my spine and into my fin. What's going on?

The electric eels swim to my father's side in front of me, and I can either go after them or help the king. I'm not sure whose side the angler fish are on, but in a snap decision, I realise the king needs me above everything else, but he's shackled to the floor. It doesn't matter how much I tug the chains, I'm not strong enough to free him.

"Use the fish," the king says to me.

"What do you mean?" I ask.

"Lure one towards the chain."

With poor sight of my surroundings, the thought sounds terrifying, despite the fact I worked with them on the light show. There's panic all around me, echoed my painful screams. I breathe in sharp gulps of water. I have to be brave and do the right thing.

Edging towards one of the fish, I whisper, "Hi, little lady. Do you think you can help me?" Her mouth opens suddenly, making me jump. I point towards the king, hoping I'm not about to lose a finger.

The sound of her teeth grating against the metal sends a shudder through me, and the high frequency attracts other fish to help. Soon, the king is free. He's not quick to swim off, and I realise it's because of his wounds. I grab hold of his arm and help him to the exit, where I find Ryn.

"You could've given me a hand. Take his other arm and help me," I say.

He does as I ask. We lead the king out of the palace and into the city square. "I need to rest," the king says.

"We can't stay here. Just a little farther," I say. "Over to the clam."

"We should head for the coral," Ryn suggests.

"Stop where you are!" someone shouts.

A deafening explosion erupts through the water, and I'm blown away from the king and Ryn. Bits of rock float by, and I cover my head, hoping I won't be hit. Unfortunately, with the second explosion, I'm covered by the rubble and I pass out.

The throb in the back of my skull is agonising. I wince in pain. When I try to get up, I can't. My tail is pinned by a large rock, and even though the dust has settled, I can't see much.

When the chaos broke out, I was with the king and...

"Ryn," I call out.

Please let him be okay. We've had an intense love-hate relationship, but I don't want anything to happen to him. It's hard to think straight because of my injuries, and my heart hurts. I can't lose Ryn. Through the good and the bad, I still love him. *Please, Gods, let him be alive.*

"Ryn!" I shout again.

Trying to sit up, I start to clear the rubble off my body. The large column pressing on my tail won't budge however hard I try. There's an iron rod nearby from inside one of the building structures. I reach as far as I can, but it's too far away. My eyes feel heavy, and I'm losing hope of being able to escape.

"Ryn," I say weakly before closing my eyes. A few minutes later, the column on my tail starts to rock. When I look up, Ryn has the rod and is trying to free me. "Ryn," I whisper.

"I'm here," he says, coming towards me.

"What happened?" I ask.

"The rebellion stopped the merfolk from taking back the city. They've taken the king."

"Oh, hell."

"We need to get you out. Do you think if I move the column, you'll be able to push it?"

"Let's try. Have you heard from my mum?" I ask.

"She's okay."

"Thank the gods."

"Hey. We won't let Neptune win. Maris will be back soon, and we'll take back our city." He cups my cheek and I pull him close. We kiss softly. "Come on. Let's get you free."

He returns to the rod, and I sit up so I can push the rock. It isn't easy, but eventually, I wiggle free. We embrace each other, frantically kissing and squeezing each other tightly.

"I thought I'd lost you," I say.

"I'm here. I'm not letting go."

My body is bruised and battered, but I'm glad to be in his arms. An overwhelming feeling of love washes over me as I realise how much I need this merman. I'm frightened and don't know how we're going to get out of this mess, but I know I need Ryn by my side.

SCORPIO
LIBRA
VIRGO
LEO

Chapter Thirty-One

AQUARIUS STANDS ALONE

Maris

Atlantis is in ruin, and I fear I'm too late. Our glorious city is no more. Instead, it's reduced to a pile of rocks.

"Hello," I shout. The waters are deadly quiet. Everyone can't be gone, can they?

I search the waters, only I can't find any sign of life. I'm glad everyone managed to escape, but I have no idea where they've gone or what's happened.

I swim towards the palace. That's when I see the first

merman. It's one of my dad's guards, and I go to him. "What happened here?" I ask.

"Maris?" he asks in shock, and a bad feeling settles in my stomach.

"Is my father okay?" I ask, although he hasn't answered my other question.

"Come with me and I'll take you to him."

I swim backwards with unease. "Where is he?" If he doesn't say the dungeon, I can't trust him.

"Where do you think he is? Cyrus is on his throne, of course."

"I thought Neptune took over the city?"

The realisation is evident in his wide eyes. He knows I'm about to flee. I swim as hard and as fast as I can.

"Hey!" he shouts.

The secrets of the city have been drilled into me since I was a little mer. The clam is badly damaged when I reach the city square, but it's the easiest way to get out of view. I open the trap door under the statue and quickly go inside. I grab a pole from the collection I used to use to play queens and jam it into the handle of the door. The guard that was following me tries to open the door, but the metal is strong and longer than the hatch, so it doesn't give way. It holds firm, and I relax against the wall. I can't get caught, especially with the jug. I need to figure out how to heal Atlantis without falling into enemy hands. These tunnels under the city are like a maze, and not many mer know they exist, never mind being capable of navigating them.

I make my way to the dungeons in search of my friends and father. It's dark in the tunnels, but I know my way. The jug is too precious to cart around, so I leave it in a safe place close to my destination. The hatch on the other side is similar to the one at the clam. Carefully, I push it over, listening to the sounds of the ocean. Once I feel the coast is clear, I swim out into the open. Lucky for me, the keys are on their hooks, and I help myself to the master. Looking through the cells, I search for my loved ones. In the end room is a beaten shell of a man. My heart sinks when I realise this could be my dad. My hands shake as I try to get the door open quickly.

"Dad," I whisper as I get closer. My voice comes out squeaky as I fill with emotion. *Was I away too long?*

Black rings circle his eyes, and his body is covered in bruises, but there's no doubt who this is. I should've been here.

"Maris? Is that you?" my dad asks in a faint voice.

"Yes, Daddy. It's me. What have they done to you?" I can't hide the horror in my voice.

"You're going to have to leave me here and save our people. I'm not going to make it far."

"Don't talk like that. Let me help you into the tunnel. We have to go."

"I'm not strong enough to stand up to Neptune."

"Maybe not now, but you will be."

"I don't have time for my injuries to heal. You need to act now and take back the city."

"And we will." I lift his arm to help him out of the cell. He winces in pain, but I don't stop. We have to get out of here. Leaving the dungeon behind, we make it into the tunnel, and I seal the entrance.

"I'm safe now. You can leave me here," my dad says.

"No. I have a better plan." I retrieve the jug from the place I hid it. The water glows like a light, and I present it to my father.

"This is Ganymede's jug. You need to drink from it."

"How did you find this?"

"Don't get mad, but I've been searching the clues of Aquarius while I was gone."

"Did you go on land?"

"Yes."

"I would be angry, but your reckless actions might be the only thing to save us."

"Drink. It will heal your wounds."

"Thank you." He takes the jug and does as I suggest. The blue liquid coats his lips, and his eyes illuminate. His skin glows with new life, and even though

I've seen the magic happen on Owen, I'm still impressed.

I wish Kasper and his brother were here to help me know what to do. I miss the way we worked as a team. I thought I could do this alone, but now the lack of support around me is making it hard. Even with my father, we're still only two people.

"Do you know the significance of finding the Aquarius treasure?"

"Yes. I've healed two souls," I say proudly.

"The flood will come, but the true leader will part the waves," he says cryptically.

"Atlantis is already underwater," I say, stating the obvious.

"The heart of the city is broken. It's divided the merfolk and literally split the city in two. It's a metaphorical flood of hate, and the prophecy says the jug bearer will bring Atlantis back together. That's you, Maris, and I'm proud of you."

"Who told you that?" I jerk my head back in surprise.

"When I was made king, the oracle gave me a gift. I've always known this day was predicted. I knew you'd save the city, I just didn't know how."

"I love you."

"I love you too. Now, let's go save the city."

"How?"

"By healing the heart."

With the jug under my arm and my father holding my hand, we navigate through the tunnels, ready to take back our city. Atlantis will be restored to its glory, and we will win back what's truly ours.

SCORPIO
LIBRA
VIRGO
LEO

Chapter Thirty-Two

Aquarians are forward thinkers

Kasper

We barely make it to the airport without the police catching us, and now the security is making me paranoid. Hopefully, it will be too late before they realise we've left Haiti. The love I have for the country will soon be a distant memory. We won't be welcome back here, that much I'm sure of.

"Do you think Maris is okay?" Owen asks.

"I really hope so. I regret leaving her behind." She's a

really special girl, and I've never met anyone like her before. Maybe I never will again. I meant it when I said I loved her, even if I didn't explain myself well.

"We should have stayed until the end."

"Her father wouldn't accept us, and he's the king of the sea. We can't exactly argue with that."

"When the doctors told you I was ill, you didn't just roll over and accept it."

"This is different."

"How so?"

"Maris and I don't have a future. I have to leave her to follow her own path, and we need to get our lives back."

"What's waiting in England for us? We gave everything up to come here."

"We'll start from scratch. You still have your computer skills, and we're going to earn an honest living."

"Do you love her?"

"Yes." I don't hesitate this time.

"Then you should fight for her."

"What about you?"

"Does she have any sisters?"

I laugh and punch him in the arm. It's been so long since I've been able to joke around with him like this.

"Maris made it so I can swim underwater without needing to come up for air," I say.

"I guess we only need to steal one scuba diving kit, then." He laughs, but I don't think he's joking.

"What if we get caught? There might be no going back if we don't leave Haiti now."

"I heard you caught some waves with some dolphins. There's always another way if we need one."

"Are you serious? Should we go back?"

"What's your heart telling you?"

"We should've decided this before we left for the airport."

"Be serious with me." He touches my arm. Now's no time to hide my feelings or what I want. I've been real since I met Maris, and that's not going to change.

"I love Maris, and I'm ready to fight for her and her city."

"Over there," someone shouts, and when I turn, it's obvious our time is up. We were never getting out of Haiti, and deep down, I never wanted to.

"Quick. We need to leave," I say to Owen.

"Right behind you, brother."

We run, and I knock over a few small suitcases. A group of security men chases us as we weave through the crowds. Our fate can't end with us in jail after all we've been through.

A staff door catches my eye, and I pull Owen into it. Off the main route, we take the long corridor, hoping it's not a dead end. The door swings open and footsteps run after us. We run down a few flights of stairs until we're in a bagging area. Without respect for the luggage, I throw myself onto the conveyer belt and start to jump over the obstacles in my way.

"Hey. Stop!" a guard shouts.

"We need to get out of sight," Owen says.

"Or at least farther in front. I think we should head up the conveyer belt and hope we can shake them."

"Where will we come out?"

"I'm hoping in the check-in lounge. Then the exit will be right there." We struggle our way up to the top as the luggage travels in the opposite direction. Some guards attempt to follow us but soon give up. We push through the flaps at the top and the bright lights are blinding. "Sorry," I say to the startled woman on the desk as we rush past her, spinning her chair. Guards are already searching for us as we surface, and we don't stop. By the time we reach the door, we have a mob chasing us.

We run out in front of a car and almost get run over. I put my hand on the bonnet to steady myself, but we haven't got time for hesitation. A horn beeps from a nearby car, and when I look at the driver, I see it's Ryn.

"Get in!" Pasha shouts from the far side.

"This is our ride," I say to Owen. I let him take the nearside, and I race around to Pasha. She has a bandage on her leg.

The car doors slam and the engine roars to life. Ryn's driving is more like a dodgem ride, but at least the security isn't following us.

"Have you driven before?" Owen asks, fastening his safety belt.

"Sure," Ryn says.

"Don't lie to him. Driving here doesn't count as experience," Pasha scolds.

"I'm trying my best," Ryn says.

"What happened to your leg?" I ask.

"My father blew up Atlantis."

"Shit. How's Maris?"

"We haven't seen her since she left with you."

"How did you know to come to the airport?"

"My human connection picked it up on a police scanner," Ryn says.

"Thank you. We might not have made it if you hadn't turned up."

"Don't thank us yet. We're about to pull you into a war."

"The moment we started looking for the jug we were already involved," I say, realising it's the truth.

I hold the seat as we turn the corner, and Pasha steadies herself, holding the dashboard. There's no time to waste as we head for the beach in search of the ocean.

"Owen can't breathe underwater," I say.

"Don't worry. I have a potion, and I will gift him the warmth of the sea," Pasha says.

"You can't kiss him," Ryn says.

"Are you going to do it?" she asks him. The car swerves to the left.

"Eyes on the road," I shout as he turns the wheel in the opposite direction.

"Sorry. I'm not kissing a human," Ryn says. He sounds unhappy rather than disgusted with the idea.

He frowns, which I can see through the central mirror. I hope this journey we've been on has opened his heart like it has mine. He never stood a chance with Maris. He might not deserve Pasha either, but maybe she will accept him, flaws and all. Love's funny in that way. He didn't seem to see Maris for her worth, whereas I already see her as a queen.

We dump the car close to a clifftop and start the decline to the beach. Pasha hands Owen a concoction that looks similar to the one I took. He drinks it without hesitation.

"Yuck. I'm not changing my diet to sea plants anytime soon," Owen says.

"We'll see," Pasha says with a smile.

"Do you think you can change my mind?"

"Definitely."

"You're on." Owen gives her the thumbs up and Ryn's scowl deepens.

He probably deserves a taste of his own medicine, even if Pasha and Owen are only teasing. Ryn doesn't stop when we reach the water, and I follow him into it so my brother has some privacy.

"How bad is the situation in Atlantis?" I ask Ryn.

"It couldn't get any worse." He seems cold with me, but we don't really know each other.

"My brother's a good guy," I say.

"I'm sure he is, but Pasha's my girl."

"Does she know that?"

He grabs hold of my shirt, and I can't help but smile. I don't mean to aggravate him, but I want to know where he stands. With him this close, it's obvious he likes Pasha.

"I've tried to tell her how serious I am, but she's struggling to believe me." His voice softens and he moves away from me.

"Things will work out for the best."

"I hope you're right."

SCORPIO
LIBRA
VIRGO
LEO

Chapter Thirty-Three

Kissing an Aquarius is like no other star sign

Pasha

"He seems to really like you," Owen says, pointing to the water.

"Ryn's a complex guy," I reply.

"I hope it works out for you."

"Thank you. You must be a special guy too. Did your brother and Maris manage to heal you?"

"Yes. I drank from the Aquarius jug and I feel like a new man."

"That's incredible!" I'm pleased for all three of them.

I never doubted Maris would make a good queen, but this is proof she's capable of great things.

"Is it time to pucker up?" Owen asks, rubbing his hands together.

I can't help but laugh. "Come here, cheeky human."

"You'll be the first woman I've kissed in years. Well, other than Maris."

My smile wavers. "Is there something between you and Maris?" I don't want to hurt her again. I struggled with my feelings for Ryn from the start, and I won't kiss any of Maris's other love interests.

"Only in the way there is between you two. She's like a sister to me, and maybe one day, she might be my sister-in-law."

My face brightens. "Did she say I'm like a sister to her?"

"Yes. She loves you, Pasha. Even if you've fallen out at the moment."

"We're still friends." I run my hand over my hair. "It's just complicated."

"You seem to like that word."

"I've never been one to take the easy route."

"You'll get there. I have faith."

"We're going to fix Atlantis. Mermaids and humans together." I step towards him, ready to give him the gift I have to offer.

The sea splashes over our feet, and I'm ready to return home. I lean in and press my lips to Owen's. The touch is soft and warm. His jaw dances across mine as his tongue explores my mouth. This wasn't supposed to be a passionate kiss, but it's full of need. He kisses across my cheek and nibbles my neck until he relaxes his forehead against mine. "Wow. I've been missing out. Do all humans kiss like that?"

"I'm sorry. I shouldn't have taken advantage."

"Ryn and I aren't officially together, but I'm not giving up on him yet," I say.

"I feel strange," Owen says.

"I'm sorry. I didn't mean to hurt your feelings."

"No, that's not it." It happens quickly, but he slips down my body and flops into the sea. Where his legs once were, there is now a tail.

My mouth falls open in shock. "You're a merman."

Owen looks panicked as he scopes the beach for people. "We'd better go." He uses his arms to pull himself deeper into the sea, and I follow. Once the water comes up to my knees, I drop into the sea and change form.

I take hold of Owen's hand and we catch up to the others.

"What have you done to my brother?" Kasper asks.

"I'm not sure what happened," I say.

“Pasha’s a great kisser,” Owen says.

Ryn’s face turns bright red as an angry scowl appears on his face. “She had no choice but to kiss you,” he spits.

“Chill your seashells. Owen’s trying to get a rise out of you.”

“You and your brother are the same. Do you think it’s okay to go after mer that don’t belong to you?”

“Hey, guys. Now is not the time to argue. Owen’s not interested in me, but we shared a kiss good enough to give me my name. Stop being jealous. There’s no reason to be.”

I swim away, leaving the guys to fall in line behind me. I can hear them bickering, but I try to ignore it.

When we reach Atlantis, there’s a blue glow over the city. It stops the arguments and silence falls over us.

“It looks like the battle has already begun,” Ryn says.

“So, what are we waiting for?” Owen asks, pushing forward.

“For Maris,” Kasper says, raising his fist triumphantly.

It’s time to storm the city and take back what’s ours. My legacy might be one of conflict, but I know what’s right. Cyrus is the true king, and my father should be outcast from the mer world. I’m going to help put things right, even if it means getting a job at the shell factory.

SCORPIO
LIBRA
VIRGO
LEO

Chapter Thirty-Four

Aquarians are compassionate

Maris

The urge to cover the city with water from the jug is strong, and I dip my finger into the magic. The blue obsidian colour covers my hand, and I scoop up the liquid. Pouring it over the clam statue, the current picks up. The seawater swirls around the monument, and like kinetic sand, the pieces shift into place.

"I always loved that clam," my father says.

"Me too." I spill more magic over the broken city.

"Stop right there," Neptune says, appearing with his army of traitors from the castle.

"I'm going to remove you from my chair, Neptune," my father says. The commanding tone stands clear, and I'm glad to have him back to full health.

"You're outnumbered and have no place here anymore. Guards, kill them," Neptune says. His men advance on us but soon pause.

"It's over, Neptune," the oracle shouts as our own people gather around. We're no longer just two mer against an army. We're a city ready to defend what's ours and our enemy doesn't look so threatening now.

"Peace needs to be restored to the heart of Atlantis. We don't need to fight. We need to talk about what will make everyone happy," I say, thinking of what I've learnt about Aquarius and my jug.

"It's too late for that," Neptune says. "Did your father tell you I want to bring the families together and get rid of the royals? He didn't want to share his responsibilities. He'd rather dictate to everyone what they can and can't do," Neptune says.

My father has always wanted things to go his own way, and I've been a victim of his overbearing rules. Ryn never wanted to marry me, and I'd have known that if my father had allowed us to get to know each other properly.

"Taking the city by force isn't the answer," I say.

"Let's go, men," Neptune says, unleashing his army on us.

I don't want this to be the way this ends. We're all mer, and we should be able to compromise. If listening to what the merfolk want could make the city happier, then that's what I want to help my dad do.

Mermen on both sides edge forwards with daggers and shields. They start to fight and disorder breaks out, creating a state of confusion. This is the opposite of peace.

I hug my jug tight as I look around at the hate. Being with Kasper gave me the confidence to dream big, and I wish I could apply it to my life under the sea. Instead of joining the fight, I swim up towards the surface. My tears fall and I scoop them into the jug. I can't allow Atlantis to crumble, but I don't know what to do.

Before I make it all the way up, I hear voices. "What are you doing out of the city?" Kasper asks, and I turn to face him, not quite believing my ears.

"You came," I say.

He moves closer and wipes away the fresh tears on my cheeks. "Of course I did." He kisses my cheek.

"I need you to help me save my family now." I lean into his body, taking comfort in his presence.

"You're stronger than you think. You don't need me,

but I want to stand by your side. I want to give you the same gift you gave me by saving your world."

He grabs my neck and pulls me into a passionate kiss. I allow water to spill from the jug into the water as I drink Kasper in. Blue crystals light up the water as they sink. "Thank you for coming back."

"It was a group effort. Ryn and Pasha saved us at the airport. Owen didn't take much convincing either. You're not alone. People and mer alike love you and will stand by your side."

"Kasper." If we're going to stand side by side in my world, I want him to know how I feel about him.

"Yes."

"I love you as more than a friend."

"I love you too." He takes my hand and kisses it before we head back to Atlantis.

I feel more ready to take on the chaos. As we drift lower into the sea, the blue obsidian lights up the water like fireflies. My father and Neptune are beating each other with their bare fists. Mermen are losing their lives all around, and Atlantis is bleeding out. My grip on Kasper becomes my anchor throughout the madness.

A beautiful green-tailed mermaid helps Ryn push back a few of Neptune's guards. I blink a few times as the familiarity of his friend comes into focus. "Is that Owen?" I ask.

"Apparently, if you drink from the jug and kiss a mermaid on the lips, you turn into a merman," Kasper says.

My eyes widen. "I didn't know that was possible."

"We will tell you all about it once we've taken back the city. I'm going to help Ryn and my brother. Stay close."

I start to follow, but a scream from Pasha makes me change direction. Neptune has a dagger to her throat, and my father is staggering forward. "Don't come any closer," Neptune says.

"You wouldn't kill your own daughter," my father says.

"No, but neither will you." They seem to be using her as a shield to divide them.

Pasha bites down on her father's arm, and he lets go. She swims over to my dad, and Neptune grabs for me. I swing the jug, which hits him in the chest, pushing him back.

"Give me the jug," Neptune says.

"No. It's time for you to leave."

He reaches for me again. Pasha and my dad move towards him as I struggle away. Pasha dips her hand into the jug and covers Neptune's mouth with it. "Kiss him on the lips!" she shouts to me.

"Why would I kiss your dad?" I frown.

"There's no time to waste, just do it," Pasha says as her dad struggles. I trust she knows what she's doing, so I let Neptune have it and plant a big smooch on his lips. I never thought I'd be doing this to a guy twice my age, but it's for a good cause.

Neptune starts to choke before he glows the blue colour of the liquid from the jug.

Did Pasha help me kill her father? I only have to wait a little longer to find out the truth. Neptune's tail turns into legs, and he can no longer breathe underwater. He's no longer a merman. He's a human.

Pasha grabs an oxygen mask and helps Neptune put it on. He can no longer speak underwater or do anything else mer can do. He starts to swim up towards the surface.

"How did you know that would work?"

"I didn't, but when I kissed Owen, he turned into a merman. I don't know if it was my desire or just what happens after drinking from the jug, but it was worth a shot."

"What if you'd transformed into a human?"

"I didn't drink from the jug."

"So, what now? We can't kiss all our enemies."

"I don't think we'll have to," my dad says before shouting, "Mer of Atlantis! Neptune is no longer part of the mer community! Now settle down or get out." His command sends ripples through the water like the true king he is, and the merfolk fall silent. It's almost peaceful.

LEO
VIRGO
LIBRA
SCORPIO

Chapter Thirty-Five

AQUARIUS MONTHS MARK THE START OF THE RAIN FOR MANY PARTS OF THE WORLD

Kasper

Maris did what she set out to do, and using the jug of Aquarius, she fixed the broken city. Calm seems to have settled over the merfolk.

"You've had your fun now, Maris. Say goodbye to your humans so we can return to the castle," the king says as merfolk start to leave for their homes.

My brother stands at my side.

"I love him, Father. Haven't you learnt anything from this experience?" Maris pleads for her father's understanding. I knew I wouldn't be accepted in Atlantis, but hearing it is much worse. The merfolk stop their retreat to watch the interaction.

"He doesn't belong here," the king says.

"Says who?" Maris challenges.

"Me," says the king coldly.

"Look around you. The merfolk want change. They want to be able to choose their own paths and have equal opportunities. I want to choose my own fate, and I'm choosing Kasper," Maris shouts loud enough for everyone to hear. She's standing up for what she believes in and he has to listen.

"Your daughter is an exceptional young woman, and I'm honoured she thinks so highly of me. I will follow her to the ends of the Earth to keep her happy," I say, declaring my intentions. If I can't be with Maris, her father can lock me in jail, so at least I'll get to see her every day.

"The jug gifted me the ability to be a merman. Kasper can be one too," Owen says.

"The merfolk won't accept him as the princess's partner," the king says, curling up his lip.

"I disagree," the oracle says, swimming forward.

The king looks around at his people as they nod their heads. These people are standing up for me. I've never felt as at home as I do here with Maris.

"Is this what you want?" The king directs his question to the merfolk.

"Long live Princess Maris and Prince Kasper," the oracle says, and the words get chanted around the kingdom.

"No. As my daughter has made it clear, times are changing and I am out of touch," the king says.

"Father…" Maris starts.

He waves his arm to cut her off. "Maris, you've shown great courage and empathy for our city. If the merfolk will have it, I'm passing my crown to you."

I look around, wide-eyed. Maris has shown all the skills her father thinks she has, but I'm not worthy of becoming the king by her side.

"Long live Queen Maris," the mer shout.

I bow my head. "My Queen, if you'll have me, I'd love to stay in Atlantis, but only as your Kasper. I don't need a title. I'm here to serve you."

"My Queen," Owen says, bowing his head.

"My Queen," the oracle says, following suit. Next to take a bow is Pasha, then Ryn, until the whole kingdom accepts her.

"I want there to be a vote in council if I am to lead. I want equal opportunity and democracy. I want to award Pasha for her bravery rather than punish her for her father's mistakes. Most of all, I want a big wedding to celebrate my love for this man, if he'll have me?" Maris says.

When I first started this mission to find the jug of Aquarius, I didn't realise I'd find so much more. Owen and I have a future now, and it's so much better than I imagined. Maris is a modern mermaid, and she knows her mind. She may have beaten me to that question, but I'm happy to give her the privilege.

"I love you, and of course I accept," I say.

Merfolk around us cheer, and even her father gives a faint smile. I go to Maris and kiss her with all I have. People around us rejoice, and he hugs us both.

"My brother's all grown up, and I'm gaining the best sister-in-law," Owen says.

"And you've also become a merman," Maris replies.

"Yes. It was kind of an accident, but I'm digging it."

"That accident is what saved us," I say.

"And it means Neptune won't come back here now he's officially a human," Maris says.

"Don't you think he'll come for the jug?" I ask.

"He can try. But he won't succeed," Maris says with confidence.

"I'm proud of you," Cyrus says, hugging his daughter. "You'd better look after her," he says to me.

"I will, sir," I tell him.

"This room is bigger than the whole apartment I owned in London," Owen says, making himself comfortable on his new bed in the palace. He's been assigned a room close to the one I'll be staying in.

"I'm glad you like it," Maris says, looking pleased with herself.

"Will you be okay in here?" I ask. I know I don't have to worry about my brother anymore, but old habits die hard.

"We saved the day, and now we're living under the sea like royalty. Life doesn't get better than this." He puts his arms behind his head.

Maris laughs. "It's good to have you here."

"I'm looking forward to having some time with my girl," I say, kissing her nose.

"Go get reacquainted, you crazy lovebirds."

We say our goodbyes, and Maris leads me to her room. She places the Aquarius jug in a vault before joining me on the bed. "Congrats, Queen Maris, on mending all the hearts, including mine."

"That's sweet."

"Not as sweet as it will be to finally taste you."

A warm blush creeps over her face as she moves

closer. We kiss softly at first, but it soon turns heated. Maris's tail transforms into legs, and I remove my shorts. She watches me unfasten her shells, and I let them slip away. We're finally completely naked together. "How may I please you, My Queen," I ask, taking in her beauty.

"Be with me, Kasper," she whispers.

I kiss down her face to her chest. Delicately, I circle her nipple with my tongue before sucking in the bud. She whimpers under my touch and the sound goes straight to my cock.

Maris is pure, and I want to make this special for her. She makes me a better man.

I move my focus to her other breast before licking down to her navel. Soft moans leave her lips as I move lower. Every curve, every groove, and every opening are mine to memorise. I want to worship every inch of her body.

Bypassing her most intimate area, I scatter kisses down her thighs and lick the soft skin behind her knee. With my thumbs, I massage down to her ankles and along each toe. Both her legs and tail are mesmerising. Slowly, with my arms stretched up, I move back up her body until I'm nestled between her legs.

She watches my every move with a lustful curiosity. I'm desperate to taste her, but I tease her outer lips. I lick along the hood of her clitoris before finally plunging my tongue into her folds. She tastes so sweet as I continue my voyage. I roam over her lips before settling over her clit. I home in on her sensitive spot. Her soft moans let me know she's enjoying my touch. Around and around my tongue goes until she's quivering under me.

"Yes, Kasper. That feels so good," she says between moans of pleasure.

Her encouragement has me working my mouth faster and faster until she screams out her orgasm.

A satisfied grin appears on my face as I move up the bed to kiss her lips. "Should we wait for our marriage before going any further?" I ask.

"I'm done following other merfolk's rules. I'm in charge now."

"I think I like this new demanding Maris."

We both smile. She brings her knees up around my hips and I line my dick up with her entrance. I take my time easing into her so she can adjust to having me inside her.

"I forgot the condom," I say, almost in pain.

"I'm hoping once you change into a merman, we can have children, but we can't like this," Maris says.

The idea of having kids should scare me, but it doesn't. I want everything with her. "You want me to become like you?" I ask.

"Yes. Don't you want that too?"

"Yes." I push farther inside her, and this time, she moans with pleasure. My next thrust isn't so gentle, and her response is to grip my ass. "You like that?" I smile.

"Don't hold back."

That's all the encouragement I need. I slip in and out of her, loving the sensation. She tightens her hold on me, and I fuck her harder. She feels better than anything.

We come together, screaming our orgasms before I collapse on top of her.

"I love you," I say, kissing her shoulder.

"I love you too."

SCORPIO
LIBRA
VIRGO
LEO

Chapter Thirty-Six

The male Aquarian may be a non-conformist

Ryn

"Damn it, Pasha! Will you just listen to me?" I say, swimming after her.

"No. It's been a long day, and I'm ready to go home."

I grab her arm so she's forced to look my way. "Then come home with me."

"I'm not doing that anymore." She shakes her head.

"Why not?" My features tighten. I haven't been the best boyfriend, but I'm going to change that.

"I'm done being your bed warmer. I want to find true love."

"Well, it's staring you right in the face," I say.

Her jaw drops open a little before she narrows her eyes. "Don't play with me."

I rub my hands over the back of her shoulder. I've never told anyone this before, but I don't want to lose Pasha, and I need her to know how serious I am. "I love you. I always have," I say, holding eye contact.

"But..."

"There's no but. I'm sorry I haven't always shown how I feel, but I'm going to be better."

"You're a royal who will marry another royal. There's no point in us dating."

"Times are changing and that's no longer true. I'll marry whoever I like, but let's not get ahead of ourselves. We never truly gave our relationship a chance."

"You're not giving me a good enough reason."

My heart sinks, but I'm not ready to give up yet. "I never wanted to marry Maris or any other royal. Now I realise I won't be rushing into a long-term commitment. I want to spend my days with you and see where it goes."

"I won't sneak around with you or meet up late for a rendezvous."

"That's not what I'm asking. I want you to be my

girlfriend, and I'll shout it from the top of the clam if it will get me what I want." A faint smile appears on her face and it gives me a sliver of hope. "Just give me a chance. I'm not promising I won't make any mistakes, but I will try my hardest to be the right merman for you."

"You have one chance." She holds her finger up, but I'm already going in for the kiss. I capture her lips with mine and pull her into an embrace.

"No more sneaking around."

"No." I take her hand and lead her towards my home.

"I thought we agreed on no late hook-ups."

"You might change your mind on that, but first, we have somewhere to be."

"Where are we going?"

"You'll see."

I lead her to the royal quarters and into the main room of my home. My sister and mother are sitting together, making pearl necklaces.

"Nerida. Mother. I'd like you to formally meet Pasha. My girlfriend." They both look up but neither smile.

"Well, I'll eat my shellfish. I didn't think you had the balls to bring her in here," Nerida says. A strangled laugh cackles in the back of her throat.

"Sorry, Nerida. You'll have to find someone else to show you off to the court."

"Did you hear? Dating a human is now all the rage." She shrugs like it's no big deal, but I can't imagine my sister overcoming her pride. She's a first-class snob.

"Enough, Nerida," my mother says, silencing us both. "It's good to finally meet the creator of the ocean carnival show. I look forward to working with you on future projects."

"Thank you," Pasha says. Her cheeks redden, and I think she likes my mum's compliment.

"I'm glad Maris appointed you on the committee." She smiles warmly.

"She did?" Pasha asks.

"Of course."

My mum and girlfriend seem to get on well as they chat business. Having everyone I love in one room feels right.

After a few hours, I swim home with Pasha.

"Goodnight, beautiful," I say, kissing her lips softly.

"Thank you for today. It meant a lot," she says, helping herself to another kiss.

"This is just the start. I'd like to take you out for Valentine's Day."

She smiles brightly. "To show me off," she says.

"No. Valentine's Day is just for us. It's a day to show you how much I love you."

"I could get used to this."

"That's good to hear because I'm not going anywhere." I drop a lingering kiss on her lips before finally letting her go.

I mean every word. I'm determined to show her we're made for each other.

VIRGO
LIBRA
SCORPIO

Epilogue

THE FEMALE AQUARIAN MAY APPEAR TO BE THE ICE QUEEN: BEAUTIFUL BUT DISTANT. THEY DON'T USUALLY FOLLOW THE GROUP, AND THEY LIKE UNCONVENTIONAL RELATIONSHIPS

Maris
One month later

My fingertips run along the buttons of the dress as it hangs against the window frame. A human dress is not what my father expected to be giving me away in, but I want to break free of old traditions.

"I can't believe you're getting married on a beach," Pasha says, peeking out of the villa window.

"The sun is shining brightly on the Florida Keys, and the ocean is the prettiest blue. What more could a bride ask for?" I say.

"You have me there. I'm envious."

"How are things going with Ryn?"

"He wants to go to France, and I'm thinking of finally accepting."

"Put that guy out of his misery and tell him how you feel about him."

"I plan to later tonight. How about you? When are you going to tell Kasper you're trying to set his brother up with Nerida?"

"All in good time, my friend." I kiss her cheek.

"Fifteen minutes," someone shouts into the villa.

"Come on. Let's get you into your dress," Pasha says.

Once we're both ready, we head to the arch, where I'm going to marry the man of my dreams. My father takes my arm, ready to walk me down the aisle. "You look beautiful. Both of you," he says.

"Thank you," we reply in unison. I'm glad Pasha and my dad have found a new understanding for each other.

The soft music starts, and we begin our walk. Kasper's wearing shorts and a dinner suit jacket, which makes me smile. It's quirky and sexy all at the same time.

"Hi," I say when I reach the arch.

"Hello. Wow. I'm a lucky guy," he says.

I smile even brighter, feeling like the luckiest girl in the world.

"Dearly beloved. We're gathered here today to

witness the marriage of Maris and Kasper," the registrar begins.

I've never been happier. Everyone I love is here with me today in a beautiful location, and I'm marrying my soulmate. We say our vows before celebrating around a campfire, waiting for the stars.

"I've got you a wedding present," Kasper says, pulling me towards the water.

"I thought we agreed not to do that," I say.

"This was too perfect to pass on." He pulls out a small box, and I open it.

"Two koi fish. It's beautiful. Thank you." The necklace is made from glass polished by the sea and seaweed.

"In Greek mythology, two koi fish represent Pisces. Legend says their tails are tied together to prevent them from losing each other."

"That's a lovely story."

"I'm never letting go of you, Maris."

We kiss passionately. "I'm not going anywhere without you."

The End

If you enjoyed this book and would like to check out the next in the series, ***Crazy in Love by Ruby Wolff*** *is now available to purchase:*

SCORPIO
LIBRA
VIRGO

Sneak Peek of Crazy in love

by RUBY WOLFF

Saylor

"You must think I'm crazy," I shout at Anika, as she holds up the tiny black piece of fabric she's calling a dress. "That's not even going to cover my ass." I push the dress out of my way so I can continue to look at the clothes.

I swear she chooses the most ridiculous outfits sometimes. Just once, I would like her to pick an outfit that would look nice on me. She must do it on purpose... I bet she does.

"That's because you have a huge ass." She gives my

ass a slap as she walks away laughing at me, while I rub the sting on my left cheek. "There must be something here you like. I mean, everything will look sexy on that fine body." She turns around, then looks me up and down, shaking her head at me.

"What?"

"You make me sick, with your perfect ass, perfect tits, perfect... well, look in the mirror." She grabs my arms and spins me around to face the mirror on the wall.

"I know, look at me," I say as we both start laughing. "I keep telling you to come to one of my classes-"

"Yeah, yeah, yeah. Sorry, yoga isn't my thing." Anika waves her hand in the air as she turns away from me. "Now, let's find you something smoking hot."

Shaking my head, I follow her around the store. She has been on my case all week about coming to some uppity work thing with her tomorrow night. I hate the rich business crap. I went to one with her two years ago, and God, it was the most boring thing I've ever suffered through, and to top it off, they serve some ridiculous shit they call food. It was not food. It was these gourmet things that just looked wrong, almost inedible. The waiter told me what they were called, and I just rolled my eyes at him. I mean, if it has a fancy name, then I know I'm not eating it.

Anika has been working so hard to finally get a job at

this company. It's all she's ever wanted to do, and if I have to go to this party to make sure she keeps her job, then I will.

"How about this?" I grab the maxi dress, which is backless, and Anika raises her eyebrows at me, then shakes her head with narrowed eyes. "Fine, you pick something. You know I hate shopping." I start moaning as she picks up a few dresses for me to try on.

"I think you're the only girl in the world who hates shopping." She pushes me into the changing room and hands me an arm full of dresses.

Rolling my eyes at her, I shut the door and hang the dresses up. Seeing if any of them take my liking, I give them a onceover. This is punishment, but the sooner I pick a dress, this nightmare will finish.

I'm one of those shoppers who knows what they want; walk in, walk out. But Anika can spend a whole day here. Trying on outfit after outfit is torture. I'm sure that is why online shopping was invented, so I didn't have to do this.

Straightening out the blue dress, I open the door. "No," she says and hands me more dresses, she's just pulled for me to try on.

How can she say no? She didn't even look at me.

I look at them, then back at her. Why has she given

me these choices? She knows I hate wearing dresses that show my ass off.

"Come on, Saylor. If I had a figure like yours, I would live in these." She shouts so I can hear her through the closed door.

Pulling the next dress over my head, I tell her, "You have a great figure, so stop selling yourself short."

She always puts herself down, and she's not even fat. I mean, she isn't skinny but not fat either, with amazing curves that I would love to show off. Some days, she will be proud of it, then some asshole will say something stupid to her and it brings her down. I keep telling her that next time a guy says anything to her, she needs to punch them in the face, or I will. No one messes with my friends, because I'm sure I have a few things to say to them too.

"And I love you for always saying that to me."

"Okay, I think this is the one." Opening the door, I stand in an off the shoulder black dress that comes to my knees, with a thigh-high split. Even though I don't like to shop, when I find a dress that looks this amazing on me, I can't help but smile.

"Oh my God, you're going to get laid tomorrow night, looking that hot," she tells me with a laugh. I look in the mirror to make sure it looks good in the back too.

I have to say, I do look hot in this. "I don't think

there is going to be any guy at the party who I would even give a second glance at. The suit look really isn't my thing. In the whole of London, there has to be someone good enough for me, for us. But they won't be at that party." I've never been into the man in a suit. I like some roughness, a little bad boy, and so far, a man in a suit, well, I've only met the boring ones. They spend most of their time talking about work, or how many cars they have, or how much money they earn in a day. I don't care. I go back in the dressing room to take the dress off, thankful I don't have to try on the countless others to find one I like.

"Well, we haven't found him yet, but it's not like I want one." Anika peeps through the door.

"Me neither. I'm a lot happier having fun." I gather my things, so I can pay for my dress. "Before you say anything, I already have shoes." We both start laughing, as we share a shoe closet and a good seventy percent of them are hers, but she never says no to me.

"You teaching tonight?"

"Yeah, want to meet for dinner after?" Paying for my dress, we head out and walk to the coffee shop to take away so we can walk around a little more, as Anika wants to get a few other bits for tomorrow night.

This is her dream company to work for, and she has to make a good impression. There is something big happening at her work, and she doesn't know the ins and outs yet, but she is trying very hard to get on the team. She comes home every night after work saying that the buzz around the office about this secret team is getting crazy, and everyone is trying to figure out what it is.

"Sure, I'll text you the place." Anika takes my bag from me as my studio is within walking distance from the shopping centre. "Hey, before you go, are you going to see Hayley?"

"Yeah, I'm going to tell her about the new place. Are you sure you're okay with my sister moving in with us?" I ask as I sit on the bench for a moment. I've asked her a few times to make sure she's really okay with her being there.

I've asked her so many times now, I've even lost count, but I know how much work my sister is, and I'm the one that needs to be looking after her, not my best friend.

"Come on, Saylor, since we've been friends, I've seen you struggle when she has one of her up or down days. I've even been there to help out, so I'm sure. I'm good with it." Anika gives me a hug, not just a quick hug either, one that lasts a little longer, almost as though she knew I needed it.

She's the best friend every girl needs in her life. When it comes to Hayley, Ankia has helped me so much.

If I have a yoga class, she will help when I've needed it. My sister was okay by herself, but ever since last year, I've been getting more and more phone calls from the doctors or the lady that lived next to her telling me that she is having a very low moment and disturbing the other people living in the apartment building.

I did tell Anika I would buy my own place, but she wasn't having any of it. So with both of us, and her dad's help, we got a really good mortgage and bought a three-bedroom house. She found one that was perfect, with a small one bedroom and living space outside, which will be for Hayley. So she still has her independence and won't fight with me about it.

The house needed a lot of work done to it, and that's where we got even luckier, as Anika's dad and brother are in the building business. They have spent six months at our place and Anika was the one telling them everything we wanted. So Hayley's space has a small living area with a kitchen, one bedroom, and a shower room. When I told Hayley about it, she was annoyed and kept telling me that she can look after herself, but she said if she doesn't like it, then she'll leave. It cost me a lot of money to get the living space nice enough for her to be happy with. That space was one place that I refused to take money from Ankia. I was the one that needed the room, not her, and after a while, she agreed. More like I didn't give her the choice.

"Thank you, right, I will meet you for dinner." Standing up, I give her a hug and make my way to my class for the day. I have three today. Two of them are with a group, and one is with a private client who I see four times a week. Sometimes she comes to the studio and sometimes I go to her house.

I will pop in to see Hayley on my way to dinner to let her know everything, mainly that we will be moved in by next weekend. I'm just hoping she is having a good day, because I'm not sure I can deal with her attitude if not.

"What time is the fancy thing tomorrow?" I ask as I drink my Martinez cocktail, which was needed. I felt like the second class just didn't want to be there today. You always get a feel in the room when you're breathing the energy; it always tells me how the class is going to go. And today, they did not want to be there.

"Six. I want to make a good impression. I really want to get on the team for this new app, which Mr. Kane is working on," Anika tells me with so much excitement.

She acquired an internship with Big Kane App as soon as she finished her last year of University. If she can get on the team for the app, then she might finally get the job she wants there.

"Well, I will do my best to big you up to anyone in a suit." I thank the waiter as he sets our food in front of us.

"Thank you. I know you hate these things, and I would have asked Jason, but he had work." Anika tries to make me feel better, but it's not working.

Jason is the lover in our group. He loves the idea of all things romantic; the happily ever after, Cinderella and the glass slipper. He has seen every Disney film ever made, along with romance movies of all genres, likes the flowers and chocolates, the sexy love notes and sweet nothings. Yes, he's gay, and I do love him even more for how open he is about it. His dad doesn't really talk to him, but his mum is an angel and loves him no matter what.

"Yes, he's already given me the dos and don'ts." I start laughing. He told me that I have to smile at everyone, and not to groan about everything. Jason gave me a very long list, which I haven't read the entirety of yet, and don't plan on it either. I got to the first ten points, then put it in my bag.

"So, did you talk to your sister about next weekend?"

"Yes, but at the moment, she's very serious about her

music and thinks she is about to go on a world tour," I say, taking a bite of my burger. I've learned to let her think her thoughts are real. I've tried to fight with her, but it doesn't get me anywhere. All it turns into is a full-on battle, of which I always lose.

"Nice. It's better than her running away from aliens," Anika remarks. I have to agree with her on that one. That was a long episode from her, and I played along. I've done this for years with her now, and I can really get a feel of who she is and when she is.

"What happened to Barry from the other night?" I ask, wanting to change the topic from my sister. I love her, I will always love her, but sometimes, I just want to have a nice meal and not think about when my phone will ring again.

"He was the worst sex I've ever had. It was so bad. Let's just say I didn't even know when he was inside me. Until he asked me if I was enjoying it." I burst out laughing, making the couple sitting next to us look over, then I apologize to them, pursing my lips.

"Please tell me you're joking?"

"I wish. He kissed like he was going to make my world explode, but his lips and tongue tricked me right into bed." Anika takes a spoonful of food and shakes her head at the same time.

"So are we looking for a man with a big dick tomorrow?" I dip my chip into some sauce.

Isn't that the dream for us all; a man who can kiss you so you feel like you're floating on cloud nine, and fuck you so you feel like you've died and gone to heaven.

"Yep, so if you find one, he's mine." Anika points her finger at me, so I know she means it.

"All yours. You know a suit doesn't do it for me. Now, if there is a man with tattoos and muscles, then I'm all there." That is my idea of someone worth giving a second look at, but the ones I've met are all assholes and that's before they meet my sister. I know it's going to be hard for me to find someone who will love me and accept that my sister is a big part of it too.

"Maybe if you meet a nice suit, then you might find someone worth your time." She raises her eyebrows at me.

"Well, so far, all the suits you've dated are even dickheads or shit in bed. At least the assholes I've dated are making me scream." I grab my cocktail, and she gives me that look, telling me to shut up. I have to hide the smile because she knows I'm right.

"I know. I live in the same flat as you." She sticks her tongue out at me, which makes me laugh.

We continue our evening talking about the party

tomorrow and which group she will be talking to more, and about this app they are working on.

I told her about my plans to add a few more classes in during the week, but I'm still seeing if it's a good idea since living with my sister is a first for me.

Acknowledgments

The zodiac signs are something I've always been interested in, and when Lizzie James suggested the Stargazing series, I was excited. I wanted to dive into a world that not only gave the personality traits of Aquarius, but also some of the legends surrounding the star sign.

I knew I wanted to write a golden fleece style book, and I'd recently watched a documentary about Haiti. The country has a rich and poor side with complete extremes. Already, the pieces were spinning in my head. The lost city of Atlantis is somewhere I'd really like to visit, and so I thought I'd take you to my version of it. Romance under Aquarius came to life as a real place in my mind, and I hope you enjoyed the way it turned out.

Thank you to Lizzie James and the Stargazing team for the opportunity to explore this world. Thanks to Melanie, my biggest cheerleader, and Rebecca, my go-to girl. They are both there whenever I need them and I couldn't do it without them. Thank you to Eleanor Lloyd-Jones for visually bringing this book to life over at

Shower of Schmidt. Last but definitely not least, thanks to my amazing editor, Karen Sanders. She always adds the twinkle to my stars. I wouldn't want to work with anybody else.

About the Author

Danielle lives in Yorkshire, England, with her husband, daughter, and tortoise. She enjoys reading, watching the rain, and listening to old music. Her dreams include writing stories, visiting magical places, and staying young at heart. The people who know her describe her as someone who has her head in the clouds and her mind in a book.

Thank you for taking the time to read my story. If you enjoyed it, please consider writing a short review.

Subscribe to her newsletter to stay in touch with the latest updates

Confessions of a Sophomore Prankster

Dirty Kisses and Conflicting Wishes

Kickflip Summer

The Heart of Baker Bay

Printed in Great Britain
by Amazon